PHOEBE

GREEN HILLS BOOK 7

PRAIRIE ROSES COLLECTION #50

VIRGINIA'DELE SMITH

———

**Welcome to the world of Green Hills
by Virginia'dele Smith**

Sadie & Sam: PART 1 - Introductory Short Story (FREE)
Book 0: My Manifesto - Short Memoir (FREE)

THE PRAIRIE ROSES COLLECTION

***Take a trip back in time with the
Prairie Roses Collection...***

Featuring timeless themes of
courage, strength, and resilience,
the Prairie Roses Collection
honors the women who came before us
with bravery and perseverance!

If you love historical romance,
you're sure to find inspiration and joy
in every one of these touching tales.

————

Multi-author collection available in digital format from Amazon.

To mothers…

*This book is very much a love story
between a noble cowboy and the spirited
young woman who captures his heart.*

*But in keeping with the Prairie Roses Collection
theme of honoring mothers, this book also
features a mother's love.*

*First, let me say, Mama in the story is
nothing like my mother, and I pray that
my two children will say the same!*

*I also hope you won't judge Mama too harshly,
as there's no more challenging, all-consuming,
rewarding job in the world. We all make mistakes in
that treasured role, and we're all doing our very best.*

1

What has been seen cannot be unseen,
what has been heard cannot be unheard,
what has been learned cannot be unknown.
You cannot change the past,
but you can learn from it.
You can grow from it. You can be made stronger.
You can use that strength to change your life,
to change your future.
C.A. Woolf

Day 1 ~ April 20, 1883 ~ close to midnight

When I close my eyes, he is there.

I avoid going to bed as long as I can, because when I sleep, I discover his dead body. Again and again.

His ghost isn't haunting me. It's living within my heart, casting dark shadows over my beautiful memories and replacing joy with sorrow.

The nightmare woke me once more. My heartbeats refused to slow to a reasonable speed; my restless limbs refused to still. I couldn't bear lying on the makeshift mattress for another moment.

Careful not to wake Mama, I crept from our covered wagon, wrapping a quilt around my body to cover my night-gown and ward off the nighttime chill. I know better than to wander far from camp, but I had to move, walk, do some-thing…anything to erase the vision, so vivid and real, from my mind.

The river along which we were traveling called out to me, promising peace. I prayed as I walked toward it, begging the Lord to exorcise the pain, to mend my broken heart.

The LORD is nigh unto them that are of a broken heart; and saveth such as be of a contrite spirit.

The fist squeezing my heart loosened a tiny degree.

Water gurgled over rocks, a soft and soothing sound in the darkness. I glanced all around and studied the sky. I was completely and utterly alone; the indigo blue of night hadn't even begun to fade along the horizon line…plenty of time before anyone in our wagon train stirred.

Giving into temptation, I pointed my toes to test the temperature.

The muscles in my leg jumped, but I resisted the urge to lift my foot from the icy water. Mind over matter, right?

Before we left Boston, I overheard a table of university-educated girls expounding on a book by a Scottish man named Sir Charles Lyell. His name sounded prestigious and caught my attention. From a table away, I ate my lunch so slowly as to be laughable, taking bird-like bites and chewing them until there was nothing to swallow — all because I listened to their conversation, hanging on every word as they debated the author's claim that as humans develop reasoning abilities, they improve their mental strength, thus leading to an *ever-increasing dominion of mind over matter.*

Surrounded by the dazzling colors of fall, energized by the

buzz of academia at an eating establishment close to Harvard's campus, and filled with hope from the Radcliffe students a mere table away, I had no idea what was coming. I couldn't have predicted that God would soon test my ability to control debilitating pain by sheer willpower.

Yes, mind over matter.

Despite needles prickling my flesh, I forced my frozen feet into the water, curling my bare toes into the squishy mud. I walked deeper into the numbing abyss. When every fiber of my being screamed to escape, I continued setting one foot in front of the other. A life lesson resided in the repetition. Over the past two months, that lesson had become my mantra: Keep walking, one foot in front of the other.

By definition, that meant I was indeed moving forward.

Even if the startling burn of frigid water failed to clear the tragic memory from my mind…

"*P*hoebe Victoria, that quilt will wait," my mother commanded. "Put down your needle and thread this instant and go get your father. Please?" What began as a directive ended as an entreaty.

"Yes, ma'am," I replied, yet I loaded twelve tiny stitches on the needle. I pulled the thread through the three layers of fabric, tempted to finish the curve of the feather motif I'd been sewing all afternoon. But I'd abandoned Mama to do all the cooking by herself, and I'd accidentally shirked one of my chores when she set the supper table without calling for me, just so I could keep working.

With an admiring look at my progress, I folded my project into a ball and stuffed it in an oversized wicker basket. Groaning dramatically so Mama could hear from the next room, I rose from the ancient rocking chair, moved closer to the parlor window to take advantage of every last ray of the day's light. My teasing grin developed into a full smile at her clucking and muttering; it was a silly game we played. I was too old for silly games, but I loved poking the bear. And Abigail Susanna Williamson loved being the mama bear. To ruffle her feathers and stall a bit more, I tidied the sitting area and lit two oil lamps to stave off the darkness that was quickly consuming the light. Then I flitted into the kitchen like a butterfly, skittering a dance as though I had all the time in the world.

"Supper smells delicious," I said, brushing a kiss on Mama's cheek as I breezed past. She murmured something about wayward young ladies who don't obey their parents. She didn't fool me, however. The lilt of her English accent, a remnant of her childhood in London, conveyed nothing but love and adoration. The neighbors believed Mama to be rigid and short-tempered because her gruff exterior hid her true nature, that of a gracious wife, a devoted mother, and an assiduous community matron.

I chuckled at Mama's response and let my thoughts drift to how I'd stitch the borders of my quilt as I dashed down the stairs connecting our second-floor home to the general store Papa owned and operated on the ground level. An intricate sewing pattern popped into my mind, and I called out to my father, "Papa, hurry! I need parchment and a pen. And Mama's threatening to throw supper to the pigs next door if we aren't at the table in—"

With a hand on the banister, I took the last three steps on a flying leap, one I'd done a thousand times before, the one that flung me around the corner and into the storeroom. "—five minutes," I finished saying as I landed light as a fairy on the stone floor, my eyes flittering over the colorful inventory awaiting the perfect place to be displayed in the shop.

Nestled and tucked behind the showroom and purchasing counter, the storage area of Williamson's Mercantile would have rivaled a hidden treasure trove, as fantastical as those featured in a Robert Louis Stevenson adventure. Every shelf held fabric and trinkets and tools. Jars of buttons, spools of thread, and bolts of ribbons and lace weighted a barrister bookcase. Dry goods, canned goods, barrels of sugar, and crates of tea tins created a maze that had been perfect for playing hide-and-seek when I was a child. Pungent cigars, woodsy soaps, and perfumed personal products scented the air. *A place for everything and everything in its place,* Papa always said, so anything and everything a person could want or need existed within those stone walls.

The storeroom was my favorite place to read, draw, sew, and simply *be.*

At least it *had been,* right until that moment of that day — when my world came tumbling down.

"Papa," I called out again. "It's time for supper."

Still, he did not answer. "Papa? Papa, where are you?"

My pulse quickened. The air felt too thick, too dank…not right.

The store had been closed for over an hour, so there were no customers keeping Papa's attention. Furthermore, he wouldn't ignore my voice. Just the opposite, really… Papa never failed to light up with joy when I came down the stairs. As a young girl with much to say, I would linger in the store for hours, chattering in Papa's ear about my day, my books, my quilts, my friends, my schooling, my worries, and my dreams. As a young woman with a responsibility to help in the business, we worked side by side, discussing literature, debating history and politics, and exploring all the intellectual topics Mama deemed inappropriate for a lady. In my childhood, Papa had told Mama, "Phoebe's fine here with me, dear…the best kind of distraction." As I got older, his indulgence grew, too… "Let her be, love. Life is about learning." In all instances, Mama answered with pursed lips, a muttered rebuttal, or a dismissing shake of her head. Then she'd sweep her skirts by Papa, close enough to brush his hip or shoulder, sometimes running her hand down his arm. I pretended not to see. But the love was there — every moment of every day.

When she veered back upstairs, Papa invariably flashed me a conspiratorial wink, asking, "Now, where were we, Buttercup?"

No, Papa would not ignore me. Something was wrong.

With slow steps, laden with dread, I followed the path between barrels and boxes and crates.

"Papa?" My voice came out timid, faint…my question as much a prayer for the man I adored as a call out to him. *Oh, please, Lord,* I begged outright. *Please let him be okay.*

I should've been more specific with my choice of words.

I should've prayed for him to be alive and healthy and well.

I should've put away my sewing the first time Mama asked.

I should've hurried down to the shop hours earlier. I should've spent the day helping in the store. I should have been there.

If I had, perhaps I would not have found Papa lying on the cold, hard floor, his head in a pool of blood, his body lifeless, his spirit gone.

2

———

There is a sacredness in tears.
They are not the mark of weakness,
but of power.
They speak more eloquently
than ten thousand tongues.
They are the messengers of overwhelming grief,
of deep contrition, and of unspeakable love.
Washington Irving

Please, God, wipe that memory from my mind.
Determined to help the Lord with my wish, I forced my legs, stiff and aching in response to the icy water, to do their job. Mind over matter.

I advanced waist-high, my nightdress billowing on the surface. I tried pushing it down, but even soaking wet, it floated around me. For some reason, its refusal to obey my command infuriated me. Why wouldn't anything *do* as it should? *Be* as it should?

In fighting with the fabric, I slid on the muddy bottom, lost my footing, and fell all the way into the river. Would my heart stop in response to the arctic temperature? Did I want it to? Sweet oblivion awaited.

Embrace the cold, the darkness…escape.

Ignoring the need to inhale, I focused on the cold, feeling it in my bones. I imagined my blood slowing as it froze. Then I imagined Mama. I envisioned her life in the West, filled with wild experiences she'd not wanted and with no one to help her through. I saw her heart breaking yet again, and I worried such pain might actually break Mama.

Pushing off the slimy mud, I gasped for air the moment my head cleared the surface of the water. After several deep breaths, my inhales and exhales returned to normal. Then came the tears.

Perhaps caused by my grief or my near-death experience, or maybe in response to the extreme cold, sobs overtook me. More than sobbing, my shoulders shook and my heart hollowed, and I cried and wailed until the sorrow turned to anger.

Why did Papa die? How dare he? How dare God?

What were Mama and I to do? How much longer could I wear my mask of optimism? Couldn't everyone around me see that nothing was good nor right? Didn't they notice me crumbling on the inside?

Why? Why? *Why?*

Fury filled my veins. Although my skin still puckered with gooseflesh, I no longer felt the chill. Without conscious decision, I slapped at the water. Then I did it again. Over and over, I battered the lapping waves I created, swiping and lashing out in the form of a violent tantrum. They're not my style, but one schooled in the art of social decorum is not ignorant to the alternative of their training.

I gave the water my all, kicking and punching and screaming until my energy dissipated and I needed to either trudge my way out of the water or freeze to death where I stood.

The former won out. With leaden feet, I marched to the shore.

My good sense returned, as did the etiquette lessons drilled into my subconscious over the past twenty-one years. A rock, flat and round, served as a perch where I sat to clean my feet and calves.

By the time I finished rinsing them, my body trembled with violent shakes. Apparently, freezing to death remained on the table.

Not willing to return to the camp in only a quilt, I wrung water from my nightdress in handfuls. It clung to me, still rather wet, yet dripping less and less with every twist.

The sound of a horse nickering in the distance alerted me to the time.

Huddled in my quilt, I hurried back to camp, climbed into our wagon without making a sound, and crawled under a heap of blankets and furs.

My body craved warmth. By some miracle, my soul felt cleansed.

Create in me a clean heart, O God; and renew a right spirit within me.
Psalm 51:10 drifted through my mind.
Thank you, Lord.

That, my last conscious thought, delivered peace as sleep, blissful and welcome, wrapped me in comfort.

Day 2 ~ April 21, 1883

*A*ctivity greeted me when I awoke a few hours later.
The night guard shuffled in for a bit of rest. Men and boys rounded up the cattle, women and children cooked

breakfast, and the campground resembled an ant colony, where every member has a role and scurries to get it done. It was our first morning on the trail, and no one wasted any time.

Mama glowered but didn't rebuke my tardiness, so I jumped into meal preparations.

She arranged wooden trenchers, tin plates, and metal mugs at one end of a makeshift buffet line constructed with two stacks of traveling trunks and a door someone hoped to salvage for their new home at their final destination. To stay out of her line of sight until my hair finished drying, I opted to fry bacon in a skillet over the open fire.

"Of course, Mr. Rawes. I can see how that route is a quicker one. On the other hand, heading south to Hackett before turning west keeps the train clear of Cherokee lands." The man speaking to Joe Rawes, the wagon master, looked a few years older than myself. The rich timbre of his voice carried to where I worked.

"And right into the hands of the Choctaw," the gristly older man argued.

"Relations between the Choctaw and the folks in this region are stable. Chief Jackson McCurtain is well-respected. His wife, known as Aunt Jane to all, is a strong advocate for peace and education for their Indian nation. The train travels safer through their lands than anywhere else they will venture. It is your decision, of course, sir. I just thought you would want to know how relations have evolved since your last trip through the territory."

I glanced up to see Mr. Rawes's response.

Unfortunately, Mama walked my way and noticed my nosiness.

"Those partaking in breakfast prefer that bacon not crumble itself from overcooking," she commented. "I'm sure focusing on your task at hand will prevent such a tragedy to befall our meal."

"Yes, Mama," I agreed, failing to control my lips from curling into a small, guilty grin.

"No more walking through the woods during the night, either," she scolded. Her smoothing a tendril of my hair behind my ear softened her command. "It's not safe like it was at home…now that we're on the trail."

"Yes, Mama," I repeated, removing the skillet from the flame. "Thank you," I added, smiling at my beautiful mother and leaning in to peck a kiss on her cheek. "I'm sorry."

"For traipsing the woods, burning the bacon, or eavesdropping on conversations which are none of your concern?"

"Must I pick just one?" I asked as I sashayed past her to set the bacon next to a big pot of corn porridge.

Mama shook her head at my antics, but she followed behind me, tinkering with the basket of biscuits Mrs. Barrett — Louisa — brought from home…well, her previous home in Springfield.

Louisa and her husband, Jude, along with their three children, eight-year-old Oliver, six-year-old Sally, and two-year-old Fredrick — called Freddie — were bound for Santa Fe. Jude's brother had already settled his family in a small community about thirty miles from town. The Wilson family— Lewis and Sarah and their four children: Frank, Margaret, Walter, and Robert, all between the ages of four and seventeen — traveled with the Barretts. They'd lived in the same neighborhood in Missouri, and the three husbands planned to open a bank, a law office, and a medical practice out west, where such professionals were still rare in remote areas.

The day they'd all arrived in Fort Smith to gather before setting out on the trail, the wagon master instructed travelers on the wagon train to form small groups of a dozen people to share duties such as cooking, erecting camp, and tearing down tents. When Lewis and Jude noticed Mama and I traveled with a hired driver but no male relative to assist us, they'd insisted we complete their travel group.

It took less than a day for them to feel like family.

At least to me.

Mama reserved judgment, as was her way. But I'd noticed her mentoring and offering advice to both Louisa and Sarah, so she'd already deemed them worthy peers.

By the time our portion of the journey ends in Green Hills, I know Mama would be sad to say goodbye.

"Phoebe, see if Mrs. Barrett needs help feeding the children, please," Mama said, gesturing with her eyes toward the young woman wrangling a less than cooperative Freddie.

I hurried over, but the man I'd seen discussing the travel route with Mr. Rawes beat me to them.

"Howdy, partner," he said to a squirming Freddie. He extended his hand as though greeting a grown man. "I'm Mr. Davis, but you can call me Henry." He spoke in quiet tones, which attracted the boy's attention even better than a thundering holler might've. "And who are you?"

"Fedtty," the boy mumbled, suddenly shy, but he reached to shake Mr. Davis's hand.

"Nice to meet you." Mr. Davis shook the boy's hand, mirth twinkling in his eyes. Even from a few feet away, his irises resembled the steel beams I'd seen used to construct buildings in Boston…thick, dark gray, but not flat. Kind, but not soft. No, the man's eyes suggested a giving heart paired with an iron will.

Shrugging off the way his eyes mesmerized me, I remembered Mama's instruction.

"Mrs. Barrett, I'm happy to take Freddie," I offered. "We became fast friends on our walk yesterday afternoon." I put my hands out to Freddie, hoping to give his mother a break.

He responded by leaning toward me. His eyes, however,

remained glued to Mr. Davis as I lifted the small boy into my arms.

"Wooof," Freddie urged, patting me on the collar to make sure I paid attention.

"I'm sorry, sweetie?" I had no idea what Freddie tried to say, but guiding him away from barking at Mr. Davis seemed like a good place to start.

"*Wolf,*" the child enunciated. At the same time, he lurched his weight toward Mr. Davis, pointing at the man's breath-taking eyes.

Mr. Davis dodged the poking finger and caught the boy in one easy motion.

"Wise little fella, aren't you," he said, settling Freddie into the crook of one arm. "My Indian friends call me *Nashoba Tvshka*. That's the Choctaw way to say wolf warrior."

Freddie garbled some letter combinations that sounded nothing like the beautiful language Mr. Davis spoke.

"Almost," he said with a chuckle. "Say it after me: *Nash-O-ba Tav-sheh-kah.*"

Freddie mutilated it once more.

"Close enough," Mr. Davis said, ruffling the boy's shaggy blond hair. "Freddie, aren't you going to introduce me to your friend?"

Dragging my eyes from Mr. Davis's face, with his chiseled jaw, tanned skin, and stubbly beard, I smiled at Freddie and once again raised my hands to hold him.

"My Pea-bea," Freddie said, jumping ship to land against my chest with a stout *thud*.

Mr. Davis gripped my elbow to help steady my stance while Freddie wrapped his chubby little arms around my neck in an exuberant bear hug. Freddie did his best to smother me. Suffocating in love is still suffocating, and I found myself straining for air a second time in one day.

"Easy, Freddie," Mr. Davis soothed in good nature. His

hand moved from my elbow to my back, again to render aid and support. Such forward behavior wasn't allowed in the hallowed halls of Boston society, but for all I knew it was commonplace for a man to rest his large, muscular, warm hand on the small of lady's back on the frontier.

I sure hope so.

"Let Miss Phoebe catch her breath," Mr. Davis added in a kind yet firm voice.

He knew my name.

3

Bee to the blossom, moth to the flame;
Each to his passion; what's in a name?
Helen Hunt Jackson

"Thank you, Mr. Davis. I—"

"Henry." He corrected me in the same insistent tone, but at a lower, huskier pitch than when he'd spoken to Freddie.

"I couldn't—"

"You can," he interrupted again. "Please? Just when no one's around," he added.

Did he envision frequent occasion for the two of us to be conversing *when no one's around?*

My heart raced at the thought.

"Well… Henry." I paused, savoring the sound of his given name on my lips. Again, such bold behavior would not have been tolerated in Boston's upper crust. Indeed, saying it aloud produced quite a thrill of excitement. What a wild world to behold once one headed west. "I should get Freddie a plate. Very nice to meet you."

"The pleasure's all mine," he said with a hint of a grin, as though concealing a secret he wasn't quite ready to reveal. Two steel lasers, his eyes seemed to see right through me — no, right *into* me, into the heart and soul of my being…as though he truly saw *me*.

What should've been an unnerving effect instead delighted me. A thought fluttered through my mind: *I could easily look into his handsome face, meet his all-encompassing gaze, indefinitely.*

"Baka," Freddie said, wriggling in my arms. "Baka, baka, baka," he demanded, flouncing on the beat of his chant.

"Yes, let's go see if I ruined the bacon as Mama predicted."

"He's an armful; let me help." Mr. Dav— Henry lifted the boy from my arms, settled him back on the same arm where he'd held Freddie before, and gestured for me to lead the way.

"What do you want?" I asked. Henry juggled Freddie and Freddie's plate, while I balanced one for Henry and one for myself.

"Everything."

He spoke of breakfast. Surely, he did.

And yet, the intensity with which he said it, paired with that enigmatic expression he wore when he looked upon me, sent a delicious *frisson* over my skin.

His mannerisms intrigued me, the way he spoke with quiet authority…the way he expressed what could only be interpreted as keen interest, but without a single display of roguish behavior. A scene played through my mind, of young women batting their eyelashes and giggling with coquettish simpering to catch his eye. Henry didn't come off as a rake, but it wasn't a stretch to believe the world fell at his feet. Pulling my gaze from his, I straightened my spine and returned to my task, adding porridge and eggs to our plates.

"You might not want the bacon," I said after a moment's consideration. "Contrary to Freddie's insistence, I might have overcooked it."

"Like I said, *everything* looks good to me."

Again, the intensity! He looked at *me*, not at the display of food on the table.

With all three plates filled, I led our little party to a tanned cow hide which lay on the ground near the campfire. The fire worked to both distract Freddie and lend warmth, and together, Henry and I kept Freddie in one place long enough for the energetic boy to consume most of his breakfast. The moment he chomped his last bite of bacon, however, Freddie was off and running. In an instant, Henry was on his feet to give chase. Before he'd taken two steps away, Henry looked back at me over his shoulder. "Thank you for the company, Miss Phoebe."

That was it. That was all he said before turning to follow Freddie. His tone insinuated an invitation. An invitation to what? Another meal together? More time in one another's company? Time when no one else would be around? As he'd said…when we could use one another's given name?

Papa had promised more than once — warned, at times — that I'd meet a man worthy of my attention, stumble upon a love worthy of my heart. Could this be the type of romance Papa predicted I would experience? What would Papa think of Henry? Considering the way he managed little Freddie without hesitation, the understated confidence Henry exuded, and the way the man's eyes sparkled when he looked my way, I imagined Papa would've thought quite highly of Mr. Davis.

Oh Papa, how I wish you were here to tell me yourself. How does one trust their feelings when it comes to matters of the heart without their most trusted confidant? Without the only guide they've ever known. Without their best friend to share the journey?

Tears threatened to fall.

I scurried to my feet and hastened to the wash station.

"Let me," I offered, nudging Margaret Wilson to go visit with the other young ladies chatting after their breakfast.

"Are you sure, Phoebe?"

"Of course. I'm happy to wash these up. You go enjoy a few minutes with the other girls before we begin today's journey."

"Don't forget, you promised to read to us again during nooning."

"I remember," I pledged.

"Chapter three… You said it's where Tom and the prince meet."

"So it is: the beginning of their grand adventure. When we stop for the midday meal, we'll eat and read together before everyone is called to chores. If you can gather them in a circle, it'll be a fun picnic for the children who want to hear the next two chapters of *The Prince and the Pauper*."

"I'll see to it. Thank you for reading to us," Margaret said. "I'm too old for children's books and library time, but I enjoyed your narration very much, all the same."

"You're never too old for a good book, even one read aloud," I assured the girl, who stood on that precipice between childhood frolicking and adult responsibilities.

She smiled in response before adding, "Well, your books are very beautiful."

The sweet girl dashed off before I found words to reply.

I treasured my book collection. Each volume held a cherished note in addition to a marvelous tale, a gift from Papa. In the front cover of every book, he penned a message. In the inscriptions, he explained why he chose that book for me to read, or pointed out the morals of the story, or detailed a bit of trivia pertaining to the author. My favorite books contained but three words in Papa's writing: *I love you.*

A tear dropped into the washtub.

Then another.

I swiped the back of my hand across my cheek. I'd tried so

hard to stave off another round of crying. Was an hour without sadness too much to ask?

My thoughts always returned to Papa's death, to my loss and my grief. Would the pain ever subside? Diminish? Would this gripping anguish ever release its hold?

The blessings of your father have excelled the blessings of my ancestors, up to the utmost bound of the everlasting hills. They shall be on the head of Joseph, and on the crown of the head of him who was separate from his brothers.

To question the Lord's plan did no good, but I couldn't stop myself...

Why, God? Why leave me Papa's blessings — his books and his stories and his wisdom — but take away my father? I need him! Here. Now.

Tears fell in earnest while I scrubbed the porridge pot with a fury.

"What will Mrs. Wilson do if you wear a hole in her cookware on day two?"

Henry spoke in soft tones from over my shoulder. Without asking permission to do so, his gentle hands pulled the pot from mine under the soap bubbles in the wash bin. Shoulder-to-shoulder, our bodies blocked the intimate scene from others' view. I stood frozen in place, determined to reign in my emotions. Henry finished washing the dishes. I moved to dry the stack with a clean flour sack; again, Henry took over without a word.

"I can put them away," I said. "I know which pieces belong in which trunk."

Henry nodded, holding out a handful of cutlery. His expression offered empathy and encouragement and was almost my undoing.

"Shouldn't you be with your family?"

"My family is the herd of cows I'm punching."

"Punching?"

"Driving," he supplied. "I'm a cattle drover."

"What exactly does a cattle drover do?" I'd heard the terminology but never gave it enough thought to wonder what that meant in the real world. Certainly, I never met any cattle drovers in Boston.

"I, with a team of cowboys, drive livestock from one place to another." His voice, while neither arrogant nor boastful, held a note of pride. This was a man who took pride in his job. No doubt he did it very well. He possessed that look of competence that some people wore like a fine-tailored vest.

"Where do you take them, your family of cows?"

"From ranch to ranch, from ranches to feed lots, from markets to slaughterhouses."

"Where they're…slaughtered?" I asked, cringing at the vision.

"To feed our country," he assured with an indulgent chuckle.

"Yes." I nodded, understanding the system and its necessity. "What about this herd? Where are they?" I asked, looking around for proof of their existence.

"They belong to a rancher who hired us to bring them home. They spent the night grazing in the area. We rounded 'em up before breakfast. Today, we'll drive them ahead of the train once we get the *Wagons Ho* from the trumpeter."

"Not *every* day?"

"No, we'll keep 'em close to the wagons when we're going through more hostile areas."

"So, Mr. Rawes agreed with your suggestion to travel south to Hackett before turning west to avoid Cherokee lands?"

"You were paying attention," Henry commented. The tilt of his head indicated I'd impressed him. "Good memory."

A wave of sadness rushed through me. As it came upon me with warning and faster than I could defend, the effect of it must've shown in my face. His playful grin fell to a flat line; his eyes sharpened, but with kindness and concern.

"Some things I wish I could forget," I told him, again fighting infernal tears.

"Be sad," Henry said, nodding his head. The gesture not only granted permission. In a crazy way, it validated my feelings…suggested that I wasn't going mad with grief, that it was okay to feel all the terrible things I'd been feeling the past two months. "Get angry," he added. "Storm and stomp and scream to release the pain. But as they say, *Don't throw out the baby with the bathwater*… Hold on to every good time and funny tale and special moment, too. Think on them, laugh at them, and don't be afraid to say his name."

"You know about my father?"

"Yes."

I waited for Henry to say more, but he didn't elaborate.

My eyes darted over his features, hungry for understanding. "How?" I asked.

"When I picked up this herd of cattle in St. Louis, a telegram was waiting for me at the sale barn. Pa sent instructions to meet up with the wagon train as soon as I could, to escort y'all to Green Hills."

"You live in Green Hills?"

"I live on the open range," Henry corrected. "My family — Ma, Pa, and my two younger sisters — settled in Green Hills almost two years ago. They've helped develop the establishment into an actual town, one able to support the needs of the folks who've made it their home."

"The advertisement Mama answered, the one looking for a shopkeeper… Your family posted it?"

"The town did, but Pa does most of the bidding on tasks like that. He worked as a lawyer back in Virginia and is the only person in Green Hills with experience reading law, so he acts on behalf of the town as an unofficial mayor."

A string of questions popped into my head... *What sort of town has only an unofficial mayor? Is it wild and ungoverned? How many people lived there? Is it even established enough to support a general store? Did we make a mistake leaving Boston? As though there was any choice!*

"Phoebe," Mama called to me from across the clearing. Her insistent tone forced my eyes from Henry's and refocused my wandering attention. I glanced around, noticing a scurry of activity as families reloaded their wagons, preparing to move down the trail. "Phoebe!" she yelled again.

"Coming, Mama," I answered, but my eyes returned to Henry's.

"You don't always travel with a wagon train?"

"No," he admitted with a shake of his head.

"You were sent *here*, to this specific train?"

"I was," Henry confirmed.

"To escort everyone to Green Hills?"

"Not *everyone*," he said in a less forthcoming way, hedging his words with a tilt of his chin as the corner of his mouth lifted in the tiniest of grins.

"Not everyone?"

"No, ma'am," he answered as his grin grew.

"You were sent here..."

"For *you*."

4

A mother's love for her child
is like nothing else in the world.
It knows no law, no pity. It dares all things
and crushes down remorselessly
all that stands in its path.
The Last Séance by Agatha Christie (1926)

"Why were you talking with that man?" Leave it to Mama to get right to the point.

"His name is Mr. Davis," I told her. "He's escorting the wagon train to Green Hills."

"You didn't answer my question," she said, disdain dripping with every word.

"Just sharing pleasantries while helping Mrs. Barrett with little Freddie," I replied, striving to sound casual and indifferent. Talking to Henry — being near him — had felt like so much more, but letting Mama in on that truth would come back to bite me. Mama would disapprove of any relationship between me and any man on the wagon train. She'd refuse my indulging in even a mild friendship, much less one that included a bit of flirtation. She'd be downright furious if she knew a man asked to call me by my given name, and an apoplectic fit would ensue if she heard me use his. Mama believed, and had stated many times and in numerous ways in the past, that no gentlemen worthy of becoming a husband existed in the Wild West. That opinion would absolutely pertain to a cow drover, one who lived on the open range and likened cows to family.

As much as I wanted to tell her all about Henry, the risk of doing so outweighed the wish to share what would undoubtedly result in nothing. He lived a life of nomadic freedom, and Mama would never grant me mine.

"Ready to put this in the wagon?" I asked, picking up a box of flour, sugar, and other dry baking ingredients.

Encouraging Mama into a supervisory role changed the subject. I lifted the rest of our crates, some heavy with cookware, and others light with utensils and linens. She added our trash to the pile of rubbish burning on the fire we'd used earlier for cooking, and I climbed under the canvas canopy to secure our belongings for travel. Leather straps attached to the wooden slats, which formed the "bed" of our wagon, wrapped around crates, trunks, and boxes. Soft items filled the center, including blankets, quilts, pillows, fur rugs, and carpetbags stuffed with clothing. Little room remained for passengers. That suited me fine; it hadn't taken long the day before to determine that I preferred walking — even endless miles for hours on end — to riding in a miserable, jarring, and horribly uncomfortable wagon. People called them *prairie schooners*, but I'd found out the hard way that wagons do not glide across the land like a boat over water.

The wagon driver Mama contracted, Mr. Bumpus, finished rigging our oxen and took his place behind the reigns just as the trumpeter called *Wagons Ho*. When we met Mr. Bumpus in Van Buren, he seemed able-bodied and agreeable enough, so Mama hired him to help us hunt for food and provide at least the appearance of protection. He liked talking to the livestock, which I found adorable, and he hadn't so much as blinked an eye at Mama's constant stream of instruction, although he'd lived on the trail for many years and Mama, prior to our trip west, never stepped foot on one. Oddly, however, they got along quite well. She'd approved of his English heritage and cringed only a minimal amount at his Cockney accent. When he'd agreed to stay on in Green Hills for sixty days to help set up the *new* Williamson's Mercantile, she'd been thrilled. Judging by the raw emotion that crossed his face when they'd discussed wages, Mr. Bumpus found their deal amenable as well…a win for both parties.

Over the next four hours, I walked, and as I walked, I strove to entertain the young ones by singing songs, hymns, nursery rhymes, and the alphabet, on a constant loop. The wagons stopped in our standard circle formation at noon, and the women and girls set out cold tack for lunch.

As promised, I read the next two chapters of the book we'd begun the day before while the children ate. Our gathering had grown. I worried that parents might be angry about the distraction, but I hoped they might also appreciate the time it allowed them to relax, knowing their kids were contained in a safe space. A few of the children, like Freddie, who were too young to follow, curled up in a sibling's lap and fell asleep.

Employing a unique accent for each character, I tried to bring the book to life for my audience. I gave the foul royal guard a hateful, malevolent voice. Tom's sounded hopeful, albeit accepting, while Edward's held a note of imperial ignorance, so foreign was the real world to the sheltered prince.

The children gasped when the guard tossed out the actual prince and their frowns darkened when the people of London mocked him. One child scoffed and several nodded in empathy when John Canty collared the young prince and punished him unfairly.

In following Tom's tale as a new prince, the children sat bug-eyed, marveling at the unlikely adventure of a ragamuffin in rich silks. My audience scoffed again and nodded in sympathy when the royal family decreed their beloved boy had gone mad in thinking he was a common beggar lad.

"Woo-wee, them boys are in a pinch," Oliver Barrett stated, shaking his head and pulling poor Freddie, still half asleep, to his feet.

"Ain't nuthin good gonna come of that," said another boy in staunch agreement.

When their expressions of certain calamity met mine, it was all I could do to maintain a straight face.

Dear Lord, please keep Tom and Edward's story on the minds of these young boys, of all these sweet children. Give them something to think about and dream about and wonder about as we travel. Put reading and learning and literature on their hearts, if not by hearing this story, by introducing another to them. And another and another, until they hunger for knowledge. Bless them with good health and happiness and success as we travel this road, and all throughout their lives. God, you already know the path you've set for them. Please let each be long and prosperous…amen.

The time spent reading to the children re-energized me.

I tucked *The Prince and the Pauper* back inside the wagon, stuffed two slices of bacon inside a hard biscuit, and ate while drying dishes for Mrs. Wilson.

An hour after we'd stopped for lunch, the trumpet sounded to resume our westward caravan. The afternoon included more walking, more storytelling, more singing, and more dust. Copious amounts of dust.

Four hours later, we stopped for the day.

Five o'clock in the evening might've been eleven-thirty at night for how exhausted we looked, gritty and dirty and rather worse for wear. Rest had to wait, though. Wagons needed unloading, livestock needed tending, and supper needed cooking.

I arranged a set of forked sticks to hold a crossbar over the fire and lit the wood to boil rice and beans in two Dutch ovens. The cast-iron pots weighed less than a traditional oven, and they worked well for preparing many different foods. Mrs. Barrett placed a metal sheet on a cast-iron grate over another open fire to bake biscuits, and Mrs. Wilson strung several pots over a third cooking setup to heat canned vegetables.

In only two days of travel, we'd found a rhythm for meal prep. I preferred a fire with the trammel across it, from which I could hang multiple pots. Mrs. Barrett found a platform fire more useful for baking, while Mrs. Wilson's older boys, Robert and Walter, enjoyed constructing a star fire for their mama. The boys used what they'd gathered along the afternoon's walk to build a teepee of sticks to start the fire. Then they placed long logs around the flame in a pattern like the spokes protruding from the center of a wagon wheel.

While we tended our pots and pans, Mama organized the door-turned-tabletop with flatware, plates, and bowls, and Margaret rinsed and salted the fresh butter. She'd milked their two dairy cows before breakfast and placed the milk in a churn attached to the wagon. The bouncing and jostling of moving down the trail had turned the milk to butter, so Margaret needed only to pour off the buttermilk — saving it to make biscuits and pancakes in the morning — before washing the butter and adding preservative.

"Perhaps Miss Wilson would like this to go with her butter?"

My head snapped up at the deep, masculine voice. Mr. Davis— Henry.

I hadn't seen him since breakfast. I *had* been looking.

There he stood, fresh from a swim in the river, while I must've closely resembled a dusting rag steaming over a fire.

Lovely.

He held out a rough-hewn wooden bowl. I glanced into it and squealed with delight.

"Honey!" I exclaimed, looking into his slate-gray eyes. "You found a honey tree today? Oh— Were you stung?" My glee turned to worry. A classmate in primary school lost her father to a bee sting when we were young. Such an innocuous event, but fatal to one with an allergy to bee venom.

"Yes, and no," Henry said, still smiling down at me, as though I wore a silk ball gown rather than pounds of trail dirt, caked with sweat, emitting what had to be a foul odor. "I saw Miss Wilson tending their cows this morning and figured she'd be serving butter with supper. Will you give her the honeycomb?"

"Shouldn't you? After all, you're the one who discovered it, extracted it, and thought to gift it."

Henry blushed. Had I not been paying attention, I'd have never noticed. But he did. The tips of his ears colored a light shade of plum.

"If you don't mind, I'd rather you do it. I'll keep an eye on your fire."

"Certainly, I don't mind. But why?" I wondered, standing from the upended log I'd been using as a chair.

Henry stepped closer to me...to hand over the bowl, I assumed. He didn't, though, and his nearness felt anything *but* casual. A blush heated *my* ears. As well as my cheeks. And my lips. Were lips supposed to tingle?

"I'd hate to give the wrong impression to a young lady. Or her mother," he added, no longer smiling. Was Henry always so direct? So unfiltered and honest? So different from the boys I'd known in Boston.

Of course, Henry Davis wasn't a boy. He was every ounce a man, rugged and hardworking, virile and strong.

"How old are you?" The question blurted out my mouth of

its own accord. Mortified, my cheeks flamed from their earlier blush to searing hot coals. My hands flew to cover them.

Henry chuckled.

"I'm so sorry," I apologized in shock. "I had no right asking such a personal question. Please, forgive me." Desperate to undo the preceding twenty seconds, I stumbled over the words. "Really, I—"

"Twenty-seven," Henry said, stopping me from making an unfortunate situation even worse with my rambling. "And now you owe me…a question."

That cleared my head.

"Tit for tat, and all that?" I asked, raising an eyebrow at his teasing confidence. He didn't answer, just smiled that same *I have a secret* grin he wore so often in my presence. "Okay," I agreed. "One answer to one question. What'll it be?"

"Spend the evening with me?"

My eyes bulged out of my head.

"Not the night," he added, clearly humored by my reaction. "The *evening*…supper, a stroll at sunset, sit together around the fire. That's all I'm asking."

My heart thundered. I couldn't conjure an answer. Apparently unaffected by my lack of response, Henry pushed the bowl of honey into my hands, still smiling all the while.

"Excuse me," he said, stepping around me. "I think I need to stir these beans." Then he sat on the log I'd been using. "Oh, and Phoebe?"

He waited until I turned to look back at him, giving him my full, if slightly addlebrained, attention.

"Ask me anything, anytime. For you, I'm an open book."

He picked up the wooden campfire spoon and focused on the hanging Dutch oven, taking his eyes off me for the first time since he'd approached.

I watched him work for a split second before snapping out

of my stupor and walking to where Margaret stood at the tail-gate of their buckboard wagon.

"This is for you," I said. "For the butter," I added, hearing Henry's words, *I don't want to give the wrong impression*, float through my mind.

"How wonderful," Margaret exclaimed. "Thank you so much!"

If talking to a teenage girl could mislead, what did talking to me mean?

"I'll whip some into the butter and save the rest for serving on the side. What a treat. So thoughtful! Where did you find it?"

She waited for my answer.

"Phoebe? *Phoebe!* Are you okay?"

"Wha— Yes, of course. It's very sweet," I said, once again tripping over myself.

"The honey…"

"What about it?"

"…is sweet?"

"I'm sure."

Margaret's eyebrows furrowed.

"Phoebe, are you unwell?"

"I don't think so," I answered. "Do I look unwell?"

"Nooo," Margaret said, drawing out the word. Her brow smoothed into the wise visage of a teenager. A big grin blossomed on her face. "You look lovely…perhaps a bit smitten, but beautiful."

At that point, *my* brow furrowed.

"Is the honey a gift from Mr. Davis?" Margaret asked. "I saw you talking with him," she added with another knowing grin.

"You did?" I asked, refocusing on Margaret. "You did," I repeated. Everyone did, with us standing in the wagon train circle clearing with only a cooking fire shielding us from the entire community. "Oh, dear."

Oh, dear.

5

*Let every action, while it is finished
in strict accordance with etiquette,
be, at the same time, easy,
as if dictated solely by the heart.
The Ladies' Book of Etiquette,
and Manual of Politeness
by Florence Hartley (1860)*

*M*ama.

I looked toward our wagon and met her gaze. Her countenance did little to mask her disapproval.

Contrary to Mama's antiquated expectations of female decorum, I'd done nothing wrong. Conversing with a gentleman in broad daylight, surrounded by dozens of people, did *not* constitute a mortal sin. Reminded of my innocence, I straightened my shoulders, smiled in Mama's general vicinity, and waved.

"How can I help?" I asked Margaret, secure in my virtue, but also smart enough to know that walking over to my cooking fire — where Henry Davis continued to monitor beans capable of boiling without supervision — would be a mistake. Biding my time for a few minutes meant I could help Margaret *and* allowed a moment for Mama's ire to dissipate.

"How much honey do you think we need for the butter? I also have some lavender we can use," Margaret said.

"A few spoonsful will be adequate. We'll set out the rest as you mentioned. How about some lemon juice, too? Lavender honey butter sounds quite decadent. Do you have any lemons?"

"Oh, no. We couldn't pack fresh fruit and herbs, only dried and canned. What about you? Do you have fresh produce over there?" Wonder tinged Margaret's voice.

"Destined for Green Hills, we're not traveling nearly as far as your family is, going all the way to Santa Fe. When we arrive, we're to open a general store, so Mama purchased space on another wagon for inventory she wanted to carry out there. I don't have fresh, but we do have a bottle of lemon juice already opened in our supplies; let me go grab it."

Time to face the executioner. Papa's voice whispered through my mind, saying, *When in doubt, make flattery your friend. It gets her every time.*

"Mama, what an attractive spread for the supper platters! The jars of wildflowers are a nice touch. Such vivid colors… Did you pick them along the trail today?"

She grumbled but then hesitated. I took it as a good sign that Mama's conscience pulled in opposing directions, trying to decide if she'd rather berate me for speaking to a male person or tell me about the flowers. Luckily, the latter — her favorite — won out. Although, to be fair, correcting me ranked rather high on her list of beloved pastimes, as well. *Only because she loves you,* Papa had told me anytime I complained.

Even on the prairies of Arkansas, his spirit filled my senses, which acted as both a blessing and a curse. I missed him so very much.

"No," she said. The last vestiges of a frown pursed her lips. "Not forty feet beyond our wagon is a grove of trees. Just past the shade it creates is a hillside full of blooms. The wild geraniums are the size of saucers. Milkweed and purple coneflowers grow in patches thicker than I've ever seen. Smell the aster." She paused for me to do so. "Is that not the most aromatic aster you've ever enjoyed?"

"Incredible," I agreed. "You know I'm partial to the butterfly weed; thank you for including it, even if it's *merely a weed*," I said, bumping Mama hip-to-hip before wrapping my arm around her shoulders. "These goldenrods are huge…quite impressive," I pointed out. "Perhaps this region of the world won't be so awful after all." That might've pushed a tad too far, so I let her non-answer go. "Hm…what are these?"

I cupped my hands around a stunning flower resembling a red disc in the center, framed with a circle of orange feather-shaped petals tipped in bright yellow. "For such striking and bold colors, their scent is rather faint," I said, after inhaling close to the bloom.

"I don't know."

What? I'd never once in twenty-one years on God's green earth heard Mama string those three words in that order.

My face must've revealed my astonishment.

Mama held up her hands in surrender. "It's true. I've never seen one, not even in a book. They must thrive with some shade because I found them growing along the rocks and the bases of the trees…thick as a blanket."

"And just as beautiful," I added. "I wonder what they are."

"*Gaillardia pulchella,*" that rich voice I'd come to recognize said from behind us. He had a habit of sneaking up on me that way.

"Also called Indian Blanket," he added, smiling at me for too long and with far too much familiarity. Finally, he turned his attention to Mama. "Henry Davis, ma'am," he said, removing his hat with his left hand as his right extended toward Mama. I held my breath, waiting to see how she'd react.

She studied his outstretched hand for an extended pause, but in the end, her ingrained manners literally forced her hand. "Mr. Davis," she allowed as they shook. How wise of Henry to refrain from a delicate finger shake, or even worse, kissing Mama's hand. She'd have eschewed him on the spot for such an offense.

"Mr. Davis," I interjected. "May I introduce my mother, Mrs. Williamson? Mama, I mentioned meeting Mr. Davis earlier; he's the one sent to escort us to Green Hills."

"Thank you for your service," Mama said, neither croaking nor choking, but nowhere near congenial, and miles from sounding appreciative.

"Happy to be here," Henry said, not at all dissuaded by Mama's cold shoulder, if based on the playful grin tugging at his full lips. Two days of wind, dirt, and sun had already chapped my lips to the point of peeling; why did his look soft and pliant? "I apologize for interrupting. Miss Williamson, the rice and beans are ready to come off the fire. Where shall I set them?"

"Oh my," I exclaimed. "I forgot about them. I'm so sorry, Mr. Davis."

I scurried toward the cooking fire, ignoring Mama's voice ringing in my mind: *First the bacon, now the beans.*

Even so, a smile split across my face.

Henry met Mama. No one died.

Thank you, Jesus, for minor miracles.

I looked over at Henry, who matched my hurried steps stride for stride. His grin mirrored mine. And then, either a gnat flew into his eye, or he felt as jubilant as I, because that exquisite man winked at me.

*W*e set the beans in the serving line, and then I excused myself from the group crowding the food table. I couldn't stand to be in my dirt-covered dress for another moment. With a bar of Ivory soap and a clean set of clothes, including undergarments, a cotton blouse, and a heavier skirt than I'd worn during the day, I snuck down to the creek and indulged in a quick bath.

Skipping supper so I could stay and play in the water held great appeal. Instead, I forced myself to dress behind the screen of tall shrubs, donned fresh socks, and slid on my boots. When I arrived at our wagon, Mama appeared occupied, eating with Mrs. Wilson and chatting about fashion trends she'd seen in a new magazine called *The Ladies' Home Journal and Practical Housekeeper.*

Since Mama appeared content, I dawdled, taking extra time to comb out my long hair and braid it over my shoulder. My disgusting clothes went into the box we'd designated for dirty laundry. I grabbed a light shawl to wrap around my shoulders and headed for the buffet, famished and eager to eat.

Like a magnet, my gaze found Henry the instant I stepped into the hub of our campsite. Within a heartbeat, his eyes lifted to meet mine. I'd have sworn they sparkled. The corner of Henry's mouth lifted, hinting at an appreciative smile, and I — a plain-looking girl, with dirty blonde hair, and a smattering of faint childlike freckles — felt beautiful.

I ducked my head, repeating my motto: *Keep walking, one foot in front of the other.*

Hard as I tried to forget he was there, though, I looked his way again.

Henry said something to the cowboys with whom he'd been talking, pushed away from the wagon on which he'd been leaning, and closed the distance between us with long, sure strides.

"Feel better?" he asked, falling into step beside me.

"Tons."

"Good," he said as we reached the food line. He picked up two plates and handed one to me. "Let's eat. I'm starving."

"You haven't had supper?" I took the plate he offered me, gaping at him. Why didn't he eat with the other cowboys?

"I wanted to wait for you," Henry answered in a soft but husky voice that made my heart beat faster.

"Thank you," I replied. My voice didn't sound quite normal, either. "That was very sweet. I'd have pushed myself to hurry if I'd known you were missing supper."

"I'd have waited all night," he countered. "I meant it when I said I'd like to spend the evening getting to know you."

"I feel like you already do," I confessed. How had that happened so fast? We'd only met early that morning, only spoken a few times in total. Somehow Henry saw me in a way I'd never detected in anyone else, except for Papa, of course. He'd seen me, flaws and quirks and all, and he'd loved me the absolute most.

I refused to get emotional over Papa's death right then. Blinking to force back the tears, I shifted my attention to gathering forks and mugs, handing one of each to Henry.

"Where to?" he asked when we'd filled our plates.

I snuck a peek at Mama…still absorbed in a discussion with the other mothers. *Hallelujah.*

Then I surveyed the grounds and noticed a set of rocking chairs sitting empty. Henry followed my line of sight, and asked, "What do you think?"

"We can always offer to move if the owners take offense," I said, lifting an eyebrow and shrugging my shoulders with my response.

"Let's do it," Henry said with a definitive nod.

"*Ahhhh,* a real chair," I said with a deep exhale as I settled into the smooth wooden seat.

Henry chuckled. "Long day, huh?"

"How far did we go?"

"Close to ten miles."

"What a paltry number," I said with a cringe. "My feet are screaming it was much more."

"Are your boots comfortable?"

"Yes, I'm just teasing. I am tired, but it wasn't a bad day. While we walk, I continually strive to devise ways to entertain the children. I've sung every tune and recited every fairy tale I know, multiple times!"

"And it's only day two."

"Too true," I said with a flair of drama.

"You're a godsend to the families — the children *and* their parents."

"I'm just happy that the young ones are doing well. Also, it's not just me corralling them. The older siblings, as well as Margaret and the other teenagers, lend helping hands through the day. I'm sure they'll all sleep well tonight."

The activity around us provided noise and entertainment, and our conversation faded as we ate. The companionable atmosphere never turned awkward, and I found myself enjoying the meal very much.

We were two of the last to finish eating. When we carried our plates and utensils to the wash area, a grandmotherly woman took them from us and shooed us away.

Men rolled fat logs close to the fires where families gathered. Those with musical talent retrieved fiddles, guitars, and banjos from their wagons. Soon, music filled the air.

Henry and I sang along for a bit. He even pulled a harmonica from his pocket to join in on a few tunes. Not surprising, Henry turned out to be impressive with the instrument.

While he played, I danced with some of the children.

When parents began ordering them to bed, Henry stopped me from sitting back down.

"Have enough energy left for a short stroll?" he asked, cupping a gentle hand on my elbow.

"Oh, I do," I began, sad I'd have to disappoint him. "But Mama—"

"Climbed into your wagon twenty minutes ago."

6

Do not hide your crazy from me,
for mine seeks company,
and comfort.
Matthew Spenser

My head swiveled toward our wagon for verification. Seeing the truth in what he said, it swiveled back to Henry.

"Did she look unwell? When she got up from the campfire, did she appear sick? It's unlike her to leave me unchaperoned."

"I'm sure she's fatigued, but she seemed fine."

"Oh, my," I said, flabbergasted.

"So, how about that stroll?"

I swallowed past a lump in my throat. I'd never known the liberty to decide something like that for myself. A walk, in the dark, with a man…one I barely knew. Was that allowed? Not in Boston. But nothing on the wagon trail felt as it did in Massachusetts. There, I'd experienced no inclination — no desire — to spend time alone with a gentleman. Here, with Henry, I wanted to very much.

Were cowboys gentlemen?

Beware judging one on the basis of wealth or appearance. Papa's voice whispered from my memories; he'd shared that wisdom the first time we read *The Prince and the Pauper* together. The moral rang true in all situations; Papa was clear on that, decrying that there could be no exceptions.

How ironic the children chose the same story from my stack of classic novels.

Henry was very much a gentleman. I'd seen the proof multiple times throughout the day. I trusted him, and his knowing that took on the utmost of importance.

"Yes," I said, over the loud beating of my heart.

Relief flooded Henry's face as he exhaled a deep breath, one he must've been holding in anticipation of my answer. Perhaps his nerves weren't settled, either.

With an encouraging nod, he offered his arm. When I rested my hand upon it, he swapped the placement, curling my hand under and around his bicep. His hand covered my fingers, flattening them against his muscle. "The ground is uneven, and clouds cover the moon. I don't want you to fall."

Unable to speak, I nodded my understanding.

Heat emanating from his arm warmed my entire body. Were all men so hot?

I did not know; I'd never been this close to one. Besides Papa, of course. But Papa was my father, not a normal man.

A giggle escaped.

"You okay?" Henry asked.

"Yes, just a silly thought about my father," I said, shaking my head.

"Good," he said with a pleased look down at me.

His encouragement meant more than it should've.

"I hope you'll tell me about him someday."

"I'd like that, too," I said in little more than a whisper.

We continued in silence for a few more minutes — me

trying to watch my step, and thankful for Henry's arm, which I leaned on like a crutch.

When a horse's whinny sounded only feet away, I lifted my head to survey where we'd walked.

"Do you ride?" Henry asked.

"A horse?"

"Yes," he answered with a laugh.

"I haven't ridden…*yet*. I intend to…learn. I mean, from what I've read, living on the plains, I'll need to be an acceptable rider. So, yes, I do ride." True, I'd talked myself into the decision, but sound reasoning was never wrong, right?

"In that case, will you ride with me?"

"On a horse?"

Henry laughed again. "Yes," he repeated. "With me, not on a horse by yourself. There's something I'd like to show you."

"Is it dangerous? To ride in the dark?"

"Sometimes, but Scout and I rode this way several times this afternoon. He knows the way."

"He's surefooted?"

"Unquestionably," Henry answered without hesitation.

"Okay, I'd like to go see whatever it is you'd like to show me."

Saying it aloud hammered home how foolishly I was behaving. Any number of people would've seen us leaving the sanctity of the wagon circle together. Someone would notice us gone for too long. Many would feel obliged to share what they saw.

Despite reprimanding myself in Mama's absence, I didn't protest when Henry whistled to Scout. Nor did I change my mind about my folly when Henry set me onto Scout's back. In fact, not only did I *not* voice an objection, I delighted in the sensation of Henry's powerful hands circling my waist and lifting me as though I weighed no more than a child.

If tomorrow Mama exiles me to a convent, tonight will have to serve as my only true adventure…might as well make it a memorable one.

Henry swung up to straddle Scout. With both my legs on the horse's left side as though riding side-saddle, Henry's body and the cradle of his arms held me in place.

Oh. My. Heavens.

"Where are we going?" I eventually regained the sense to ask.

"To the top of this trail," Henry answered.

Scout's gait, slow and steady, rocked and lulled until my eyelids refused to stay open. My head, too heavy to hold erect, fell against Henry's chest. I couldn't say how long we rode like that, Henry an upright model of chivalry, and me a life-sized rag doll.

"We're here," he whispered in my ear.

I unglued my eyelids and blinked until my vision focused. Henry dismounted, and I stretched to straighten my spine. When he lifted his arms to hoist me down, I let my weight fall forward, trusting he'd catch me.

And he did, keeping a hand on my lower back until I proved I wouldn't crumble to the ground without his support.

Henry stepped back, and I scanned our surroundings.

We stood upon a flat rock, high above the campsite.

Even with clouds distorting and filtering the moon's light, I saw every detail of our wagon train, circled in camaraderie, unity, and defense. The people milling about the camp looked small from that distance, and yet I made out and followed their movements with ease. Mr. Barrett tended the fire I'd used for cooking while Mr. Wilson repaired a cracked board on the side of his wagon. In violation of Mama's contract, Mr. Bumpus smoked a pipe while checking on our oxen.

Don't worry, Mr. Bumpus. I won't tell.

No, I didn't have *any* room to talk or tattle on anyone.

"What is this place? Where are we?" I asked.

"This is our lookout spot for the night."

"Where the night watchmen keep guard?"

"Yes. Silas over there is on duty until midnight." Henry nodded toward a cowboy about thirty yards away, sitting so quietly that I'd assumed we were alone.

"He sees everything," I said, turning in a circle to survey the land. Not only could he see someone — or some*thing*, like a wolf or a black bear — approach the wagons, but he would also notice someone walking around the campsite, running into the woods…swimming in the creek.

"Was someone up here before supper?"

"No," Henry answered. "Guards patrol the area on foot while we're all awake. During those hours, every man is paying attention, alert to danger, and aware of our surroundings."

"But someone watches over the camp from a high point like this from sundown to sunup?"

"Yes, in four-hour shifts from eight p.m. to four a.m."

"Every single night?"

"Yes."

"Do you take a shift?"

"Yes, every other night from midnight to four. Tonight is my night off to rest."

I swung to face him. I bit my lip— I gnawed on it, actually, as I processed what he'd revealed. Tears, this time from anger and embarrassment, blurred my vision, but not enough to hide the knowing expression on Henry's face.

Clueless on how to proceed from the suffocating truth that Henry saw me losing all control in the river, I turned away, intending to walk back to camp.

"Phoebe." Henry grabbed my wrist before I'd taken a step, but not with force, and he didn't turn me to face him. Instead, I stood looking over the trees and hills and prairie to his side. Although darkened by night, the outline of branches, the roll of the land, and the sway of grasses blowing in the breeze were as clear as day.

"You saw me," I said in a faint, injured voice. "This morning— Or, last night— Whenever it was, I know it was past midnight." My voice broke; my chin fell. How exposed and scraped raw I felt, knowing he'd seen my outburst, such a vivid embodiment of the madness I'd been experiencing since discovering Papa's body.

"I didn't mean to," Henry said softly, so his words didn't reach the cowboy on duty. His hand, still wrapped around my wrist, slid down to my hand. Part of me wanted to scoop up what remained of my pride and dignity and run for the hills. A larger, maybe stronger, part of me wanted to cling to his hand gripping mine, to wallow in the comfort he offered.

"I couldn't sleep…the nightmare. It woke me and I had to get out of the wagon, away from everything. I needed to breathe. I couldn't. Not after walking under the stars, not after testing the frigid water. Nothing helped; the images in my head were too much. I just lost it. I— I thought I was alone." My rambling explanation lost steam; my words faded away.

"You were. And no one could begrudge the grief you feel."

"What did you see?" My temper flared. I'd been traipsing in the river, kicking and screaming like a banshee, and he'd watched. Worst of all, Henry had carried that scene with him throughout the day, throughout every conversation and interaction with me. Perhaps *that* was the secret behind his smile, the smile I'd thought so genuine and true.

"A woman — a strong, gorgeous, passionate woman — letting go…finding her resolve and fighting back against a heavy burden she's carried by herself for too long."

Like a Jacob's Ladder toy tumbling between its ribbons, my anger slipped away as swiftly as it came upon me. The frayed thread holding my emotions snapped.

Henry stepped closer. When no space existed between us,

he wrapped me in a hug. Standing at the top of the world, where we could see everyone, yet no one could see us, I fell apart in his arms.

Body-wracking sobs overtook me. The more I shattered, the tighter his grip. I'd have hit rock bottom without his support.

Or maybe that *was* rock bottom. Perhaps risking my reputation and Henry's respect for a few minutes of solace in a near-stranger's embrace amounted to the deepest level I could plummet in a pit of hell.

If, indeed, I'd discovered the lowest point, did that mean the road ahead led uphill? Of course, traveling uphill brought with it a set of challenges. I prayed those hurdles wouldn't hurt quite so much as Papa's death.

To Henry's credit, he mumbled soothing words and stroked my hair without attempting to stop my cataclysmic emotional breakdown. Even when the crying jags lessened, he continued to hug me, engulfing me in the shelter of his strength.

A final shudder of emotion caught on my breath. Henry ran a hand over my hair one last time, then slid his hand to cup my jaw and neck, pressing my ear to his heart.

It sounded steady and unmovable. Western dime novels offered romanticized cowboys who led stoic, solitary lives while saving damsels in distress and curing the world of evil. I'd enjoyed reading them purely as entertainment, never imagining such a man existed in real life. Henry proved every stereotype of a frontier hero to be true.

When I'd collapsed in his arms, mine folded between us, my hands had closed into fists.

I uncurled them, not to push Henry away, but to feel…*him*, I suppose. My palms absorbed his heat through his linen shirt; my fingers touched the skin at the hollow of his throat.

He swallowed against them, and my fingertips itched to

trace the column of his neck, to test the texture of the stubble along his jaw.

I looked into his face, seeking permission, I think. For what, I wasn't sure.

Henry tilted his head down to meet my gaze. His arm around my back remained in place, but he dropped the hand cradling the side of my head. Immediately, I missed the connection, but then he clasped my hand and fingers, the ones enjoying the feel of his skin. Henry brushed them across his lips and dragged them along his cheek, as though he'd read my mind and discerned my need to explore his chiseled features.

He brought our clasped hands to his heart.

"I'm sorry," he said. "I'm sorry for your loss and sorry for your pain. But I'm not sorry we're here. I'm not sorry I saw you in the river. Please don't be sorry, either."

I dropped my gaze to the wall of his chest, but Henry released my hand and tipped my chin back to look him in the eyes once again.

"Phoebe, you never have to hide from me."

7

You can tell if someone's into you.
You can feel the chemistry.
Bradley Cooper

I thought of no words in response to Henry's vow, and he didn't seem to need any.

Tucked close to his side and shielded from Silas's watchful view, Henry led me to Scout and lifted me onto the horse's back. I settled into the hollow of Henry's chest, once again cradled for our trek back to camp.

Emotionally spent and bone-tired, I fell right to sleep.

A distinctive whistle sounded close to my ear, followed by voices, Henry's and another male. I heard their conversation, but try as I might, I couldn't climb my way out of sleep…

I s she okay?" the voice not belonging to Henry asked.

"I'm gonna get her settled under their wagon; grab some blankets and my bedroll, please," Henry said.

"Her mother might believe she spent the entire night there, but not everyone in camp is as easy to fool. People like to talk."

"I better not hear a single comment," Henry threatened.

"I'll spread the word," his companion promised. "Or you could settle her here. Let the gossip take care of things for you."

"I'd never do that. Not to Phoebe…not to anyone."

The other man scoffed before saying, "I've seen the way you look at her…goofy grins and all. Talked about her nonstop on the drive. Shoot, you've smiled more in the past twenty-four hours than I've seen you smile in as many years."

"I'm not arguing that," Henry answered.

"Trail weddings happen all the time; you could be the first on this journey."

"It'll be a lucky man that marries her, but I won't trick her just so I can be him. Will you help me, Josiah?"

"Yeah," the man agreed. "I'll make her bed, and I'll make sure nobody disparages her name. I'll even lend you a shoulder to cry on when you regret letting her go tonight," he added, as though he thought Henry a tremendous fool.

Day 3 ~ April 22, 1883

I awoke with a start, panting and terrified from my usual nightmare: Papa bleeding out, all alone in the shop. Running my hands over my face and down my sides, I discovered I still wore my supper dress. Then I felt around and found that I laid on the ground, atop a heap of wool blankets and covered with a canvas bedroll.

The evening came back in a tidal wave.

I didn't dream it, not the revelation on the hilltop, not the tumultuous emotions, and not Henry's conversation with the unknown man. It had all happened.

Much more could have. I thanked the Lord that Henry possessed all the qualities of an honorable man.

My heart hadn't led me astray; Henry Davis was one of the good guys.

The fact brought a smile to my face.

I didn't dare get up to walk off the nightmare, not with a cowboy watching my every step from above. Instead, I rolled to my side, snuggling into the warm bedding that smelled of the earth, and horses, and Henry.

When the trumpeter bugled the wake-up call, I hurried to fold Henry's blankets and set them aside before Mama questioned their origin. Sleeping under one's wagon wouldn't raise red flags — most of the travelers slept there instead of confined inside stuffed — and stuffy — wagon beds. Mama would even understand my sleeping in a full set of clothes from the night before. On the other hand, Mama would wonder why I'd not pulled our own bedding from the wagon, and that conversation I hoped to avoid.

To the wagon master's deep displeasure, the families comprising our wagon train voted to take off Sundays for church, laundry, hunting and rest. Because of that, the bugle had sounded at six a.m. instead of four.

That also meant that instead of preparing breakfast in the dark, the sun shone in the April sky, casting thick rays of light with elegant grandeur, while I whisked pancake batter and cooked them in a skillet.

A gentle breeze blew through the trees, creating a soft whispering song. Birds chirped a good morning tune. Cattle *moo'ed* in the background. Children offered greetings with soft, sleepy voices on their way to start chores. The world awoke and came to life all around me.

What a beautiful day.

Whistling while I worked, I presented the image of someone with nothing to hide.

I kept my head down, focused on making breakfast, and my eyes refrained from searching the campgrounds for Henry Davis.

Wouldn't that have made tongues wag?

With an internal monologue, I schooled myself to *not* think about him. Remembering the way he'd held me and carried me, the way he'd cared for me? That path led to a trail of trouble.

Listing all the reasons Henry Davis wouldn't want to be tied down by a relationship, followed by all the reasons Mama would never allow him to court me, did little to keep my brain from conjuring images of his short hair, cropped and a unique shade of light brown, or the stubble of his beard over his smooth skin, or his confident smile. I really liked his smile.

Not envisioning said smile, I created a towering stack of pancakes, with a pat of sweet butter layered between each. Cooking in a skillet over an open fire came with the distinct struggle of maintaining constant heat. Somehow, I'd done just that, resulting in fluffy, golden-brown flapjacks.

Next, I stirred rolled oats, raisins, and dried fruit into a boiling mixture of milk, water, and brown sugar. Most of the families brought less flavorful porridge; the oatmeal would serve as a Sunday treat.

Just as I moved to lift the heavy pot from the flame heating it, the determined subject of my rebel mind appeared.

"Can I help?" Henry asked, not waiting for my reply. He removed the towel from my hand to wrap the hot metal handle and carried the pot to the food table.

Those three little words, in his rich timbre, sent my heart aflutter.

Good grief.

I carried the pancake platter and a heated pottery jar of maple syrup and followed Henry to breakfast.

I avoided looking toward Henry while helping the ladies put the finishing touches on the meal. With dedicated intention, I chatted with Margaret and Mrs. Wilson and anyone else within earshot while fixing my plate. I ignored the man to the best of my abilities…a veritable model of complete indifference where Henry Davis was concerned. Thus, I couldn't have been more in tune with his every move if we'd been paired in a three-legged gunny sack race.

I had shaken out a thick quilt, spreading it out under a shade tree. Better to be safe than sorry in case Mr. Moody, a preacher traveling with his wife on the wagon train who volunteered to lead services along the journey, got on a long-winded topic. He'd announced, "According to Matthew 18:20, *For where two or three are gathered together in my name, there am I in the midst of them*, so I'll begin the sermon directly after breakfast is served." He never mentioned how long he planned to preach, and the sun turned brutal if one found oneself stuck out in it. I'd left my Bible, a hymnal, and my prayer journal on the quilt while I'd gone to cook.

I invited Mama to join me there, but she'd chosen to listen to church from the comfort of a rocking chair we'd brought from home. She preferred staying close to the wagon with other ladies she'd met in the group, and Mr. Wilson strung a canvas canopy to shade them.

On my own and carrying my breakfast with a mug of hot tea, I sat down on the quilt, arranged my skirt, and leaned back against the tree's thick trunk. That's when I discovered two extra books on my stack of belongings.

The Pathfinder by James Fenimore Cooper, volumes I and II.

I looked all around, but no one paid me any mind.

How odd.

Setting them aside to pick up my plate, I studied the covers.

A gold gilt frame, decorated with a bow, arrow, and tomahawk in each corner, outlined the scarlet-red Morocco leather. Additional blocks of gold gilt designs decorated the spines. *What superb binding.* Papa would have adored them.

Someone must've dropped them or left them there while getting their food. They'd be back to claim them soon.

I returned to my plate, nibbling on a pancake while fighting the urge to be nosy.

When I couldn't stand it another second, I opened the top book. Emerald green watered silk lined the endleaves, and the title page showed the volumes' publication date: 1840. Forty-three-year-old books in pristine condition? Someone loved and cared for them very much.

I checked the inside pages of the first book for a name or notes, any clues as to who left them on my quilt. The second volume offered no hints, either.

I tried to finish eating, but the books mesmerized me.

A treat in hand calls for consumption, Papa liked to say.

I glanced around once more. Since no one appeared to need me, I dove right in.

...a just appreciation can be formed of the wonderful means by which Providence is clearing the way for the advancement of civilization across the whole American continent.

I grinned, thinking the text an apropos topic when journeying along a wagon trail.

I'd just finished reading the preface when a shadow cast over my shoulder.

With his body blocking the sun, Henry's silhouette could've been the inspiration for an artist's masterpiece. His relaxed posture, outlined in the brilliant reds and golds of a bright new day, contradicted the robust stability of his stance.

"May we sit with you?" he asked.

"We?" I countered.

"This is Josiah, Charlie, and Silas; they work with me,"

Henry said, gesturing toward the three men beside him. "We thought we'd see what the preacher has to say."

I looked past Henry's impressive form to see his companions.

I scrambled to my feet to introduce myself, even if two of the three — *technically* — knew me already.

"Please, join me," I offered. Then, I scanned the grounds to see who was watching. But no one seemed to be. In fact, many people shared their blankets and chairs with others, all visiting with one another over plates of food and cups of coffee. With a sigh of relief, I settled back in my spot.

In succession, each one of the cowboys tipped their hat my way and, stiff as a stuffed turkey, folded themselves onto the quilt. They sat toward the front edge of my quilt, keeping their boots off the fabric and leaving space for Henry to sit closer to me.

"Thank you," I said…quietly, so my voice wouldn't carry. "For last night," I added. "I'm sorry—"

"Don't apologize," he said, interrupting me with a patient but decisive tone. "Not to me, and never for being yourself."

Not wanting to say thank you again, I only nodded in response. What a gift he gave, offering to take me as I am.

Then a sly smile touched his lips, and he leaned closer to whisper, "You've been avoiding me this morning."

In the two days we'd spent on the trail, the young boys had put a lot of effort into snaring rabbits. Just then, I commiserated with one I'd seen caught.

I couldn't very well deny it. I *had* been avoiding him and I was accomplishing my goal — physically, at least. Mentally, I'd failed at an exemplary level.

"After…well, after yesterday, I thought it might be prudent to appear less…attached," I said, tiptoeing through my explanation.

He studied me without an ounce of apology.

"Miss Williamson," he said, catching me off guard with his formality. "I rather like appearing attached to you."

Mrs. Moody, the preacher's wife, saved me from having to respond. Bless her!

"If you're able, please stand to sing with me," she said. "We'll begin with *Safe in the Arms of Jesus*."

I'd no more than shuffled my skirts aside to untangle my shoes from them before Henry stood over me. With a gleam in his eye, he offered his hand to help me up.

Courage or cowardice?

What am I made of?

He raised an eyebrow, as if I wasn't fully aware of his dare, challenging me to be so bold in front of everyone. Including Mama.

I swallowed my nerves and laid my hand in his.

The instant our palms touched, everything we'd shared rushed over me. Intrigue upon noticing him, the fun in meeting him, the joy in our flirtation, interest in our discussions, the unmistakable attraction between us, and the comfort I'd found in his arms… Every emotion and every sensation he'd prompted scurried across my flesh.

Henry felt it, too. The storm clouds in his eyes and the way his jaw ticked gave him away. My fascination wasn't one-sided.

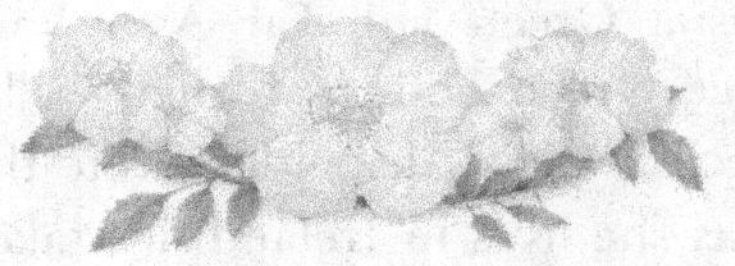

8

But they that wait upon the LORD
shall renew their strength;
they shall mount up with wings as eagles;
they shall run, and not be weary;
and they shall walk, and not faint.
Isaiah 40:31

Free from the blight of sorrow,
Free from my doubts and fears;
Only a few more trials,
Only a few more tears.

The lyrics hit home with as forceful a punch as did the air sparking between Henry and me.

We both turned to face the Moodys and added our voices to the choir.

Neither released the other's hand.

Next, we sang "It is Well with My Soul." I'd never heard a more moving rendition. Because everyone knew the words, their voices rang out with confidence and conviction. A ragtag group of strangers from various regions and a vast range of backgrounds came together in perfect harmony. We must've rivaled the Mormon Tabernacle Choir Papa had read about in *The Boston Journal.*

"Blessed be," Mrs. Moody exclaimed. "I'm not sure we can beat that." She paused for the crowd's chuckles to subside. "For our last song before Mr. Moody's lesson, I'd like to share a hymn that might be new to many of you. It's called 'There is a Green Hill Far Away,' which I thought appropriate since Green Hills is a town we'll visit along the wagon trail. Cecil Francis Alexander wrote the song over ten years ago, but as she lives in Ireland, it's taken some time to find its way here to America. It's a lovely hymn. I copied the words over as many times as I could before we left our home in Fort Smith; please, share the sheets amongst you as we sing."

> *There is a green hill far away,*
> *Without a city wall…*

A lyric sheet made its way to our quilt by the end of the first verse.

Silas held it out for our group to see, with Josiah and Charlie to his left and me to his right. We squeezed together so everyone could read the words. Henry stepped to my other side and placed a hand at the small of my back to steady me, sandwiched in the middle of the tall cowboys. His doing so struck me as the most natural courtesy.

In response, I smiled up at him as we sang.

He answered with an infinitesimal wink.

> *O dearly, dearly has He loved,*
> *And we must love Him too,*
> *And trust in His redeeming Blood,*
> *And try His works to do.*

"Amen," Mr. Moody said. "I can tell you that our singing has delighted the birds, the deer, and the angels on high. What a blessing," he added.

People shuffled paper and children and hats to sit back into their chairs, balance on logs, or lounge on blankets and quilts.

"Mrs. Moody asks that you keep those hymns. She's got a trunk full of such music she's eager to share along the trail, and I'd sure rather unload an empty trunk over a full one when we reach Santa Fe."

"Would you like to hold onto our copy?" I asked Silas.

"No, ma'am," he mumbled, either too shy or too embarrassed by my emotional breakdown at the watch guard spot to look me in the eye. "I reckon it'll only get dirty and torn in my pack."

"Josiah? Charlie? What about you?" They both shook their heads and studied their boots. Were they afraid of me? Did I do something wrong?

"Henry?" I asked, forgetting to use his last name after knowing only the first names of his friends. "What is it?" I hated to consider that his companions might think ill of me.

"Anyone ever told you that you sing like an angel?" His hand remained on my back while his other took mine to help me sit on the ground.

"What?" I asked, stupefied by his comment.

Henry waited until I'd gotten comfortable. Then he scooted beside me and stretched out his long legs.

"They don't need a sheet of paper to remember the hymn, nor the way the words sounded standing by your side. That's a gift none of us will soon forget. Wow," he said, shaking his head.

"Let's talk about hope…about steadfastness. We'll begin in Romans, chapter twelve," Mr. Moody said. I opened my Bible on my lap and flipped to the correct page. Henry leaned on one hand and shifted in my direction to share my Bible.

"Starting in verse nine and ending with verse thirteen… *Let love be without hypocrisy. Abhor what is evil. Cling to what is good. Be kindly affectionate to one another with brotherly love, in honor giving prefer-*

ence to one another; not lagging in diligence, fervent in spirit, serving the Lord; rejoicing in hope, patient in tribulation, continuing steadfastly in prayer; distributing to the needs of the saints, given to hospitality. Now, Hebrews 6:19 defines hope as *an anchor of the soul, both sure and steadfast.* And 1 Thessalonians 1:2–3 calls us to recognize the steadfastness of hope in relation to faith. These aren't easy days, my friends," he admitted. Several *Amens!* testified that many in the group agreed. "We're likely to face challenges on this trail, hardships and maybe even heartbreaks. But God— Isn't that a mighty phrase… *But, God.*" Mr. Moody paused, a talented orator and engaging preacher.

He used the remainder of his lesson to encourage not just hope and steadfastness, but also prayer, unity, kindness, and good works. Mr. Wilson gave a closing prayer, and then Mr. Rawes announced our schedule for the upcoming week. He planned to cover another ten miles per day. Barring any catastrophes, we'd be in Green Hills in nine days.

So many miles. So few days.

I looked forward to seeing our new home; I dreaded saying goodbye.

9

The wild hawk to the wind-swept sky
The deer to the wholesome wold;
And the heart of a man to the heart of a maid,
As it was in the days of old.
An excerpt from The Gipsy Trail
by Rudyard Kipling (1904)

"Mama, the laundry's hanging on the line," I announced a few hours later. "While it dries, I'm going fishing with the Wilsons."

"Is that a jest?" Mama asked with a deadpan expression.

"No," I said with a laugh. "Mr. Wilson said the more poles we man, the more fish we'll have for supper."

"And you intend to catch the fish, kill the fish, and then butcher the fish with a knife?"

"Granted, Robert and Walter made the task sound more appealing than you did. I'd wager the reality of fishing lies somewhere between their romantic description and your…less romantic one." Mama *hmmm'ed* at my teasing. "What will you do while I'm at the creek?"

"Louisa asked me to help with some baking."

"*Oooo*, something to go with supper?"

"A blackberry cobbler, I believe. And bread to have prepared for the days we're traveling."

"Well, have fun," I instructed, stuffing a handkerchief and the first volume of *The Pathfinder* into a small reticule. Then I draped my picnic quilt and a thick wrap over my arm.

"Will he be there?" she asked, stopping me in my tracks.

"I'm sorry?"

*A*t the conclusion of Mr. Moody's sermon earlier that day, families lingered to visit and children struck up games of tag. Henry had folded my quilt and walked with me to place it with my Bible, hymnal, and journal, and the mysterious novels in our wagon. Mama's observant eye followed us around, but she'd not said a word, not about Henry and the cowboys sitting with me during the church service, not about his helping me by the cooking fire before breakfast, and definitely not about the time I'd spent with him the previous evening.

By the time the church crowd dispersed to their areas of the wagon circle, women worked on lunch preparations. Meanwhile, the men compared tools, helped one another with various repairs, and checked livestock.

"Phoebe, do you mind arranging these fillings to go with the bread?" Sarah Wilson had asked from the chuck box at the end of their wagon. She'd folded down the long side, creating a worktable connected to their food storage cabinet. A mound of leftover bacon, hardtack, smoked meats, and jerky covered the center of the table's surface. Dried fruits, wild berries, and fresh apples sat alongside cooked potatoes, tomatoes for slicing, and raw carrots, filling the remaining space.

"I'm happy to," I'd told Sarah. "We have a sizable wooden board we can use as a tray, if that's okay with you."

"That's perfect. Thank you," Sarah called over her shoulder as she dashed after young Frank.

I'd returned from retrieving the tray to find Henry snacking on a piece of dried jerky...

"*I* believe that's for the nooning meal," I teased.

"Won't be here," he mumbled around the bite he'd just pulled off.

I stopped to look at him.

"It's Sunday," I said.

"To cows, every day's the same as the rest," Henry pointed out. "We'll be back before supper, though. Will you miss me?"

"I doubt it," I answered, straining to keep from smiling.

"Oh, really?" He poked my ribs — just playing, of course. As luck would have it, Mama picked that exact moment to come around the wagon.

Mama never lost her temper. She believed doing so belied etiquette and good breeding. Instead, she expressed anger in silent ways, such as the look Henry and I received.

A book I read back in Boston used the phrase *spit nails* to describe the main character's state of mind when incensed with rage. Used in a sentence, *Mama was so furious, she could have spit nails!*

"Henry, let's go," Josiah called across the campground, just in the nick of time.

"Mrs. Williamson," he said, greeting her with a tip of his hat.

"Mr. Davis," Mama replied through clenched teeth.

"Phoebe," he said, turning my way with a big smile.

"*Mr. Davis,*" I said right back, with big eyes and deliberate emphasis.

He only grinned bigger and jogged off to catch up to Josiah.

Since then, Mama and I prepared, ate, and cleaned up lunch. We sorted and repacked food boxes and cleaned the wagon. And we sat side-by-side at the wash tubs scrubbing laundry.

In that amount of time and throughout those activities, Mama had spoken fewer than a dozen sentences to me.

Spit nails might've been too cheerful a phrase.

"Will he be there?" she repeated, controlling each word.

"Who? Mr. Davis?"

"Playing ignorant doesn't suit you," she said. "And neither does acting coy."

"I wouldn't know where Mr. Davis goes," I replied. As one might guess, and unlike Mama, I had few qualms about letting my emotions fly. Deep breaths helped keep them contained. "I offered to help Mr. Wilson and the kids fish down at the creek; that is where *I* will be."

"You do too much for the families…acting like an unpaid nanny."

"Mama, this trip is arduous for you and me, and we are responsible adults with the funds to make this journey as comfortable as it can be. Lending a hand to families with small children is the very least I can do."

"You corral them all day long. Word will get around Green Hills, and the townsfolk will see you as nothing but a governess, one minuscule step above a schoolmarm."

"I'd be proud to work as an educator in any setting. Sharing literature and knowledge brings me great joy."

"You might be forced into it at the rate you're going. No decent man in search of a wife considers a nanny with loose morals an eligible candidate."

A light breeze could've blown me over.

Dumbfounded, I looked at Mama like I'd never seen her before.

She didn't mean it. I knew she didn't.

The journey, even only three days in, taxed us all. Fatigue and uncertainty affected every person in unique ways.

On top of that, her grief over Papa's death had to equal, if not surpass, my own. The only difference? Mama would internalize her pain until her own dying breath.

Once I'd blinked away the shock induced from her harsh speech, I forced a pleasant smile onto my face.

"You don't have to worry about me, Mama; I'll only marry for love."

I said it kindly, striving to sound sincere.

"It's what you and Papa shared, and I'll settle for nothing less," I added before brushing her cheek with a light kiss and walking away.

Tears, my constant companion since Papa's accident, made an appearance the instant I stepped from the wagon circle.

Be sad, Henry had advised. *You never have to hide,* he'd vowed.

I let the tears fall as I walked to the creek. Thankfully, they'd run their course and my cheeks were dry by the time I found Mr. Wilson and the children preparing sticks with fishing line and bait.

Robert and Walter — expert fishermen, of course — taught me how to cast, pointed out everything I needed to do differently, and cheered the loudest when, after two full hours of not even a nibble, I got a bite.

"Ha," I exclaimed. "I got one! I got one," I repeated, jumping up and down on the shore.

"Reel it in… Don't let him get away," the boys yelled, coaching in their own exuberant — not terribly helpful — way.

"I'm trying," I hollered right back.

"Perhaps I could be of assistance?" a deep voice asked, catching me unawares and in the throes of a sticky situation… as usual.

Henry!

He talked me through the steps to secure the fish on my hook, to give it line to help it tire, and finally to pull in my catch.

"Look! It's so pretty," I said, admiring the magenta line along its side and black polka dots covering its skin.

"And big," Mr. Wilson said, just like a proud papa. A pang of sadness pierced my heart; I acknowledged it, and then I gave the pain permission to float away.

"Easily five pounds," Henry added.

"Is that good?" I asked.

"For a rainbow trout? Very," he said, eyes alight with laughter.

"Now what?" I wondered, delighted with my success.

"Are you sure you want to keep him?"

"As opposed to…?"

"Releasing him."

"It took me over two hours to catch him," I said in disbelief at his suggestion. "Why would I put him right back in the creek?"

"So you don't have to kill him," Henry said, his tone softening. "It's okay if you don't want him to die." His patience and kindness revealed how much he understood me.

I nodded, stalling to think through what he'd said.

I swallowed and licked my lips, chewing on the bottom one while I debated my decision.

"It's part of life, though…right? I mean, God created the fish, and the Bible tells several stories of fishes feeding God's people."

"That's true." Crouching on the shore, Henry held the fish by the mouth, letting water flow over it.

"I want my catch to do that, too. It will benefit the families, and I want to be a blessing to them." Mama's words, spoken in anger, flitted through my mind. Life was hard; if I could make a moment — even one simple supper — better for another, I would.

Henry stood. Then he walked right up and kissed my cheek.

Robert *eww'ed* and Walter gagged.

"You've done the hard work," Henry said. "Why don't you relax under that big shade tree, and I'll see to the fish?"

"I brought a new book to read, if you're sure you don't mind."

"Not a bit," he promised. "Give me a few minutes to clean this fella for supper, and I'll join you."

In less than half an hour, he did just that.

As during the church service, when he sat on my quilt, he took care to keep his boots off the fabric.

"You can remove your boots," I offered.

"Never," he said, stretching out to lie on his stomach close to me.

"Never?" I questioned, lowering my book.

"Only for as long as it takes to bathe and put on new pants. Are you cold?"

"No," I answered. "Why do you keep your boots on all the time?"

"It's important to be ready *at all times*. Can I use this?" he asked with a yawn, bundling my wool wrap, pushing it under his folded arms, and laying his head upon the pillow it made.

"Ready for what?" I asked. A soft snore answered me.

I returned to my book.

It was a wonderful tale. The author's wisdom, shared without judgement or rancor, impressed me.

...as Providence rules all things, no gift is bestowed without some wise and reasonable end.

I'm gifted with the children; it's not boastful to recognize. I enjoy their company, and they seem to have fun learning and exploring with me. The ability to interact and entertain them is a God-given talent. As such, it *should* be used to some wise and reasonable end. Let them call me a nanny, a governess, or a schoolmarm; I'll wear the labels with my chin held high.

Again, I pushed away the argument with Mama.

But in the next chapter of *The Pathfinder,* our disagreement resurfaced.

Such consaits will come over men, from long habit — and prejudice is perhaps the commonest failing of human natur'.

"Precisely!" I blurted.

"Huh?" Henry's head popped up.

"I'm so sorry; I didn't mean to wake you."

"Lewis and the kids still fishing?" he murmured, still half asleep.

"Yes, I hear them squealing."

"Good. Give me ten more minutes."

I flipped through the pages of the book, counting how many until the end of the chapter. Seeing I would need more than ten minutes to finish the chapter, I marked my page with a small remnant of quilt fabric and set aside the book.

I indulged in the pleasure of studying Henry in his sleep.

His taut and firm features had relaxed, making him look more childlike. My fingers itched to feel the coarse whiskers covering his cheeks and jaw. Giving in to temptation, I smoothed his brow. Once I'd touched him, I couldn't seem to stop.

My fingertips traced his straight eyebrow. My nails ran

through his hair. When I ran my hand across his cheek, he clasped it as he'd done on the rock.

My heart raced when, also as he'd done before, he brushed the back of my hand across his soft lips.

"You are the best form of torture," Henry said, before setting my hand on the quilt and pushing up with a groan. He sat next to me, rubbed a hand through his short hair, and then set his hat on his head.

That softer, more casual version of Henry did something to me. He was adorable.

"You can't look at me like that," he said, voice still rough and raw from his nap.

"Like what?" I asked.

"Like *that*," he answered, which was no answer. "Not here. Come on; let's walk."

A thread of guilt snaked across my conscience when he tucked my hand into the crook of his arm… Mama would not like me spending time with Henry, particularly not strolling as though courting in the Boston Public Garden.

But we weren't the only couple snatching precious time together on a Sunday afternoon, not when every one of us knew the days ahead promised to be grueling.

Are we a couple?

I didn't voice the question. I liked what we were and wanted to enjoy our time without forcing decisions…some that I, for one, wasn't ready to make.

"What were you reading?" Henry asked.

His innocent inquiry opened the floodgates.

I rambled and chattered and talked his ear off.

By the time the trumpet sounded for all to return to camp, I'd told Henry all about finding *The Pathfinder* and the marvelous tale of action, adventure, and love that Fenimore wrote. We discussed other books and the importance of educa-tion. I shared with him my story of eating lunch *almost* with the college girls from Radcliffe. Henry talked about the Choctaw tribe around Green Hills, detailing Indian affairs, the unjust treatment of the Native Americans, and how leaders like Aunt Jane — the wife of the Choctaw chief — were living in harmony with the settlers.

In the final twenty yards before we arrived at the wagon circle, the most regal creature flew over us.

"Is it an eagle?" I asked.

"A red-tailed hawk," Henry said.

"Look at that wingspan," I said, marveling at the bird's splendid glory. It circled again.

"You're in luck," Henry commented. "He sees something he likes."

"Us?"

"He seems to like you."

The hawk did, indeed, seem to fly just for my delight.

"He's remarkable…like strength in motion," I said, amazed at how the hawk glided and swooped.

"He's a ruthless hunter when he sets his sights on something."

"A bird of prey?"

Henry nodded.

"A good omen, too," Henry said.

"Really?"

"The Indians and Christians both assign spiritual significance to hawks. Different tribes believe the appearance of a hawk foretells specific things, positive things. And the Bible references hawks as a symbol of guidance… *Doth the hawk fly by thy wisdom, and stretch her wings toward the south?* Job 39:26."

"That's impressive!" Commending his knowledge caused a slight coloring on the tips of his ears again. It had an endearing effect over me.

"I spend lots of time on cattle drives, with limited reading options. I've read the Bible cover to cover more times than I can count."

"I love that," I said. "And I'm jealous. I don't know it as well as I'd like, and I'm embarrassed to confess that with so many books out there I'd love to read, I don't revisit His word as often as I should."

"If that's your worst sin, I'd say you're doing just fine."

"Oh, it's not. Just ask Mama," I said with a laugh. "She'll be happy to share."

10

The secret of your future
is hidden in your daily routine.
Mike Murdock

We returned to camp, I to my laundry duties and Henry to do whatever drovers do when not driving cattle.

Like the other evenings on the trail, the women prepared and served supper around six o'clock. After the meal, they cleaned up while children played and the men smoked, talked, and tended to chores.

Then we gathered in small groups or around fires, listening to tales and playing music. Couples danced and the married ones often snuck into the night for cherished privacy.

At eight o'clock, the first night guard began his watch. That signaled the day's end and prompted folks to settle into their beds.

Four hours later, the night guards changed shifts.

Henry watched over the camp; his presence up there evoked in me a sense of security.

Day 4 ~ April 23, 1883

A dream rather than a nightmare woke me. I gauged the sky to guess the time. The fainter stars disappeared before my eyes; soon, we'd hear the bugler's call.

I'd again slept under the wagon, wearing my clothes for the new day, and didn't hesitate to crawl from my blankets to stroll through the morning twilight.

Water's song, trickling over stones and tripping through reeds, led me to the creek. It begged for companionship.

I set aside the quilt I'd wrapped around my shoulders and removed my boots and socks. After circling one ankle and then the other, I wiggled my toes like a musician tickling the keys on her piano and then planted one foot on a steppingstone covered in an inch of clear water... *Ahhh,* much warmer than the river in which I'd frozen.

Keep walking, one foot in front of the other.

With my skirts gathered at my calves, I made a game of locating the next perfect rock on which to step. Again and again, I chose a destination, trained my eyes on where to land, and leaped with faith. Silly, childlike freedom developed with every hop.

When — and why — does one abandon the youthful activities that bring such joy?

Over time, worries and stress replace innocent ignorance. Trials and tribulations lessen the amount of laughter in one's life, replacing smiles with the difficulties of adult life.

The Lord giveth and the Lord taketh away.

The bugle sounded from camp, interrupting my musings... time to start another day.

I'd meandered farther upstream than I'd meant to, so I hurried to get back to my belongings.

Henry and I reached them at the same time. He looked

good in the pale light of dawn…tired after his guard shift, but still *really* good.

"Good morning," he said, extending a hand over the water to balance my last step to shore.

"You found me," I said, clasping his hand with a soaring heart. Yes, the Lord giveth.

"I seem to have an internal radar where you're concerned," Henry said, leading me to a small, flat boulder and lifting me to sit upon it.

Without asking, he pulled a handkerchief from his back pocket and began drying my feet. He rolled each sock over my toes and up my ankles. Then he slid on a boot, rested my foot on his knee to lace it up, and repeated the process.

The decadent pampering — *wholly inappropriate* — warmed every inch of my being, not just my feet.

Henry lifted me off the rock as effortlessly as he'd set me up there and unfolded my quilt to drape around me.

"That's okay. You've chased away the chill."

"I hope so," he said. Henry's voice reflected his sincerity.

"In more ways than one," I added, matching his tone.

He wrapped my hand in the crook of his arm, as he liked to do when we walked.

Our stroll back to camp ended before reaching the wagon circle. It wouldn't do to arrive from the pasture together first thing in the morning.

Henry placed a chaste kiss on the back of my hand, and we went our separate ways.

*E*ach day repeated the last…
    I saw Henry at breakfast, and then he disappeared for the day.

Cooking, cleaning, packing up camp, and walking filled my morning hours.

Cooking, cleaning, reading to the children, and walking filled my afternoon hours.

After we made camp, Henry would reappear, fresh from bathing in whatever river, creek, or pond we'd stopped near.

In that space between setting up and cooking supper, he'd find me with a group of children, sometimes playing games and other times sneaking in life lessons such as cooking or cleaning…each a desperate attempt to keep them safe from harm along the trail.

No matter our activity, Henry joined in.

"*W*hat have we here?" His rich baritone voice startled me one afternoon.

"Girls' work," eight-year-old Oliver Barrett grumbled, displaying his displeasure at my choice of hobby for the day.

"That's perfect! I'll be right back," Henry said, jogging with a loose gait toward the temporary corral where Scout grazed on native grasses. He returned with a bundle of clothing and, sitting cross-legged like the children, wedged his way between me and Elise Jenkins, a sweet twelve-year-old whose pregnant mother sent her off to play most hours of the day.

If it weren't for the broad shoulders, tall frame, and his innate masculinity, Henry could've been one of the young boys.

"This is missing two buttons," Henry said, shaking out a blue cotton shirt. "This sock needs darning, and these denim work pants have a tear in the knee."

After sharing his mending pile with the group, he untied

the strap of a small leather pouch, unfolding it to reveal a tidy needle case.

"Miss Phoebe, do you have any thread close to this color that I could borrow?"

Henry picked up the shirt and held out his palm to display the two buttons he intended to sew back on.

"I do, Mr. Davis," I said with delight. "Here is my thread. Please help yourself." I handed him a cookie tin I'd repurposed to hold bits and baubles and sewing supplies.

"Mr. Davis, you know how to sew?" Oliver asked with a look of abject horror on his cherubic face.

"Of course," Henry replied. "Every cowboy knows how to sew. When I'm out punching cows, there are no women around to help me with domestic tasks. Yes, sir, a genuine cowboy has to be self-reliant. They know how to cook, and clean, and even how to sew." He turned his focus back to his task at hand.

I resisted the urge to comment or even smile while Oliver watched Henry.

The boy contemplated what he'd just learned for several moments before asking, "Miss Phoebe?"

"Yes, Oliver?"

"Could I also borrow some of that thread?"

"Of course," I answered, delighted by the boy's decision. "I have a nice variety of threads that will go with your quilt square."

"A quilt?" Henry asked, awe in his voice. "That's not an easy project."

"Yes," I agreed. "The children are each designing a block to make a baby quilt for Elise's new brother or sister."

"My block is going in the center," Oliver informed them with pride.

Henry and I shared a grin over the children's heads before returning to our sewing.

I fielded questions, helped with technique, and *ooo'ed* and *ahh'ed* over each block.

"What do you think?" Henry asked, just as the children did. He held out the breaches he'd repaired for me to inspect.

"I'm impressed, Mr. Davis."

"Henry," he corrected. "We're the only two left."

I looked up from my project, surprised to find he was indeed correct.

One by one, the children had finished their sewing, shared their work with the group, and skittered off to play.

As a group they played nearby on the hillside, but for all intents and purposes, we were all alone.

"Your stitches are lovely," I told him. "Even more beautiful was the way you helped Oliver. It might seem insignificant, but you did good work here today…improved the boy's life."

"And that of his future wife," Henry added with a chuckle. "May I see your work?"

He scooted even closer to me and looked over my shoulder. I continued to stitch the pieces together.

"Is this part of the baby quilt?"

"No, it's one I'm doing in my father's memory. I cut the fabric from his shirts. Mama says there's no room for sentiment in a covered wagon. I disagree; I've seen families cart furniture, pianos, portraits, and all kinds of cherished mementos in and out of their wagons each night."

"That's true. As the days pass, though, some of those items will be discarded. What seemed important in the beginning loses value over time, especially as life and death decisions arise."

The thought tugged at my heartstrings.

"I've seen remnants of people's lives along the trail already," I admitted. "I couldn't bear to throw out all of Papa's things, couldn't imagine never seeing them or touching them again."

"What happened to your pa?" He'd no more than whispered the question, and yet the weight of it stole the oxygen from my lungs.

"I'm not exactly sure," I said when I'd found my breath again. "Our best guess is that he slipped carrying inventory boxes in our general store. He must've hit his head. Such a freak accident… One moment he was downstairs tending the shop as always, and the next, he was gone."

"You found him?" Henry guessed.

"Yes," I said with an agonizing exhale.

"Oh, Phoebe." He wrapped an arm around my shoulder. "That's the nightmare."

"Yes," I confirmed with a sob.

He pulled me closer. My head dropped to his chest. I cried. Not as tumultuously as in the river, or the hilltop, or many times over the previous two months, and the tears dissipated within a few minutes.

Reluctantly, I lifted my face to look into Henry's eyes.

He wiped moisture from my tears and ran his thumb across my cheek.

"Thank y—"

He covered my lips with his finger. Then his hands framed my face, sliding into my hair as he cupped my neck.

My eyelids slid shut; my mouth lifted toward his.

Just when his lips should've touched mine, a gunshot sounded in the distance.

"Oh," I cried, startled from the beautiful moment we were sharing.

"Let's get the children back to camp," Henry said, shifting gears far faster and smoother than I did.

"Yes. The children," I stuttered, scrambling up to my feet.

Henry scooped up my sewing supplies and took hold of my hand, dragging me behind him as he gave the children clear and direct orders.

We wrangled them into the protective circle of the wagons, out of breath from running, but whole.

Gasping for air, I looked around for something amiss.

Instead of a tragedy, however, a celebration greeted us.

The shot we heard felled a buffalo that had wandered too close to camp.

A team of men waving gruesome-looking knives volunteered to field dress the carcass. Another group offered to construct a frame from which the body would hang to be butchered. Women also jumped into action, listing stew ingredients they could share and modifying meal plans.

"I need to go check the herd," Henry said, still holding my hand. "You okay?"

I nodded, although my head buzzed from the emotional extremes I'd experienced…from delight to sorrow to…whatever that moment with Henry was…to fear…to confusion.

"This is a good thing," he told me. "It provides a protein-rich food source for a week or more, which stretches supplies and guarantees more meals for those going on to Santa Fe."

"Yes. Yes, of course," I said, shaking off the fog. "I should go help, too."

"Hey," he said, tugging my hand and turning me to face him when I'd moved to walk away. "I'll be back soon, and perhaps we can pick up where we left off."

A beautiful grin blossomed on his handsome face.

"Oh," I expelled, swallowing and blinking, but not managing a coherent response.

Henry chuckled, squeezed my hand, and dashed away.

I didn't see him for three days.

11

A human being is only breath and shadow.
Sophocles

Day 5 ~ April 24, 1883

Nearing the end of *The Prince and the Pauper,* the children begged me to finish it, so I read to them throughout most of the day, even the hours spent walking. I'd barely finished the last line of the conclusion when the children began begging for another story. *The Pathfinder* came to mind.

I'd finished reading the first volume and started the second. They needed the valuable counsel and beneficial wisdom, but I worried that with some so young, the children might find the narrative patterns difficult to follow. I made a mental note to give it more consideration.

Instead of partaking in evening revelries after supper, I sequestered myself in our wagon and the small space I claimed as my own underneath it. My ears strained to hear Henry's rich baritone voice, sneaking up behind me as he often did when I least expected him.

Sadly, I never heard it. .not while I sifted through my book trunk, in the end choosing *Alice's Adventures in Wonderland* by Lewis Carroll for our next read-aloud novel…not while basting the baby quilt, since the children had finished stitching their blocks together…and not while pining for him, reading *The Pathfinder* by candlelight.

No matter how hard I wished for Henry to appear, alas, he did not.

When the camp settled for the night around eight p.m., I'd already climbed under my covers and fallen asleep. It was Henry's night to take watch, so I knew where to find him come four a.m.

Day 6 ~ April 25, 1883

Torrential downpours threw a wrench in my plan.

When the bugler called the travel party together at six a.m., Mr. Rawes announced we'd shelter in place for the day and then we reviewed the tornado safety plan.

I spent the day reassuring Mama we'd survive, praying my false bravado into prophecy.

For hours, we hunkered down in the wagon, under the *somewhat* water-resistant canvas cover.

At one point, the wind stilled in the chartreuse sky. Not a single blade of grass moved. Was time frozen? Several of us crawled from our wagons, marveling at the phenomena, such a stark contrast to the high winds buffeting us without ceasing up to that point.

"It's the eye!" someone screamed.

"Take cover!" another man yelled.

With just that second's notice, chaos replaced the calm.

Men bellowed instructions to their families. Women shrieked and begged.

Clothes, ripped from a drying line, danced in the air.

Tumbleweeds and twigs twirled through the camp.

Standing in the middle of the wagon circle, my hands flew to the sides of my head, shielding my ears against the roar of a train bearing down through the heavens.

My hair and my skirts whipped around me.

Thick dust, heavy as a sheet, both blinded and suffocated me.

"Mama!" I yelled, knowing no one could hear over the ear-splitting cacophony.

Please, Lord, protect her.

A child wailed. Or perhaps an animal made the bawling noise.

Please, Lord, keep them all safe.

The storm strengthened.

I folded at the waist, fending off plants and debris slicing through the wind.

A vortex pulled me upward, so I crouched into a tight ball, pushing my weight into the earth.

Then, as instantaneously as it came, it was gone.

I blinked at the sunshine and slowly stood to my full height.

I turned in a circle, my eyes searching for— I didn't know what for.

Assessing damages, perhaps? Looking for lost souls?

Desperate to see Mama. Pleading for Henry.

"What did you do?" someone asked, staring at me from across the campground.

"What? I didn't— I—"

"She saved us," a woman shouted as lightning crackled and thunder reverberated in the distance, following in the tornado's wake.

"No," I started.

"I seen her do it," a boy close to Oliver's size, said, pointing a finger at me. "I seen her stand right thar in the middle of the storm."

"No," I tried again. "No, I—"

"How'd you do it, Miss?" an older man asked.

"Was it prayer?" another one demanded.

"What did you say?" a young mother questioned. "What did you promise God?"

"Nothing. I don't— I didn't—" I turned in circles, trying to make sense of the crowd closing in on me.

People I'd broken bread with, sang with, and fellowshipped with became strangers.

Their barrage of questions continued, mixed in with ludicrous accusations and insane conjectures.

"Please," a different young woman begged. Dropping to her knees in front of me, she laid a limp body at my feet. "Please put hands on my daughter. Please! Save her."

Shaking my head, I kneeled to look at the girl.

I had no healing powers, no ability to work miracles, no skills to help her.

Yet, I did — not through divine intervention, but through Papa's insistence that he and I learn first aid in case an accident occurred in the shop. *Oh, the irony.*

The storm hadn't injured the child. Her face, as blue as the clear sky, showed signs of choking.

Lifting her under the arms, I circled my arms around her, making a fist at the soft tissue under her heart.

With all my might, I jerked against her, driving the ball of my hands into her abdomen. I did it again and again, until on the seventh thrust, a hard candy dislodged and flew from her mouth.

The girl took a gasping breath, broke into tears, and jumped into her mother's arms.

"She brought her back to life," someone said, quietly, as though subdued by sheer astonishment.

Pandemonium erupted.

Day 7 ~ April 26, 1883

Once I'd escaped the frenzied pioneers and found solace in our wagon, Mr. Moody had used the tornado near-catastrophe and the choking near-tragedy to justify an impromptu sermon on miracles and how only the trinity of Father, Son, and Holy Ghost performs them.

But as for me, I would seek God, and to God I would commit my cause— Who does great things, and unsearchable, marvelous things without number.

When he'd concluded, Dr. Abbott, a young doctor also en route to Green Hills, explained how choking occurs when the throat muscles constrict around an object obstructing one's airways. By freeing the object, he elaborated, I'd opened the girl's airways. I was *not* a miracle worker.

Even though Sarah and Margaret promised people had come to their senses, I'd refused to leave the wagon.

My hardheaded decision resulted in a fair number of bruises after constant bumping and jarring while the train traveled all day. Downed trees and limbs across the trail forced men to clear the path ahead of the wagons, forcing us to go slow. From the safety of my covered wagon, I'd heard Mr. Barrett say we'd only covered eight miles that day.

"Get out of that wagon and help prepare supper," Mama ordered, flipping down the chuck box table to gather spices from our supplies. "You got lucky acting like a fool in the middle of a natural disaster, and any number of people could've aided that child. Stealing candy from another family's wagon! Why, she should've been scolded...soundly," she muttered. "Now it's time to get over yourself."

Leave it to Mama to put the world into perspective.

"You're right."

"Of course I am."

I didn't argue. During Henry's absence, Mama warmed up to me again. She hadn't forgiven me for choosing to spend time with him, but the longer she went without seeing him, the more congenial she became. Throughout the day, she'd initiated a few conversations and even un-pursed her lips, which counted as a smile for Mama.

Buffalo stew still comprised every meal, but no one minded as the delicious aroma of it simmering over a weak fire filled the campground each day, and the hearty soup of meat, broth, and a plethora of vegetables filled hungry stomachs.

Mrs. Wilson had baked apples and cornbread to make that evening's meal different from the earlier nooning meal in some small way.

"How can I help?" I asked, announcing my return to civilization.

A crowd swarmed me, but precious children made up the mob rather than half-crazy adults, so I welcomed the hugs.

Miss Phoebe this and *Miss Phoebe that* flew at me from all three hundred sixty degrees.

"Can we start our new book?"

"Can we finish the quilt?"

"Can we play with your art supplies?"

Can we, can we, can we...so much energy!

"How nice to be missed in such a brief amount of time," I laughed before addressing every one of their concerns.

Caught in the children's contagious enthusiasm, the evening hours flew by.

I'd hardly blinked and the din of camp noise silenced for the night.

It felt as though I'd just closed my eyes when a unique whistle jolted me awake.

Day 8 ~ April 27, 1883

I rolled from under the wagon, folded a quilt over my arm, and walked toward the majestic boulders bordering camp. I hadn't seen anyone perched on them standing guard, but they loomed over the valley.

Henry must be there.

Halfway between the wagons and the giant rocks, a shadow stepped into my path.

I covered my mouth to keep from screaming in alarm.

My other hand flew to my chest, calming my erratic heart.

"You shouldn't come to me at night; I shouldn't want you to," Henry's voice scratched, as raw as I'd ever heard it.

"I missed you," I confessed, flying straight into his arms.

"I've missed you, too." He rested his cheek against the crown of my head while folding me into his chest. "Come on," he said after we'd hugged for several minutes. "I found the perfect spot to watch dawn break."

We wound through the boulders. I mimicked Henry's foot placement, and he helped me navigate the climb. We reached the top of a rock just as the horizon line faded from sooty black to deep ocean blue.

We snuggled close to one another, wrapped inside the quilt I'd brought.

"Where have you been?" I asked.

"Nowhere near as exciting as you," he answered, grinning down at me before turning serious. Of course, news traveled fast along the wagon train's grapevine. "The next time a tornado's close by, please — for me — take cover."

"It was the craziest thing… One minute I'm admiring the stillest air I've ever felt, studying the sky to label its odd colors, and in the blink of an eye, the storm swirled around me, coming and going in every direction."

"That's how quickly they develop out here. There's no safeguard against when or where a funnel will drop and no guessing where it'll go. Next time you notice that putrid green sky, get somewhere low, like a ravine — *not your wagon* — and hunker down until you're sure it's gone."

"I will," I promised. "I pray I never see another tornado."

"You will. Living in Green Hills, you will. Stay safe."

"I will," I pledged. "Where were you during the storm?"

Henry shared what he'd been doing the previous few days. He told me they'd moved the cattle south to keep them safe, and he talked about how they'd been working extra guard shifts around the clock.

Elijah believed a small party of two or three men followed the wagon train.

"Are they rustlers? Or Indians?" I asked.

"If they're aiming to steal cattle, they're taking their own sweet time about trying. Indians would either make themselves known or disappear; creeping along behind us serves them no purpose."

"Except to eat a ton of dust, I'd imagine."

"True enough," Henry said with half a laugh. "White men might be dumb enough to do that, but not the Indians. No matter who they are, we'll keep an eye on 'em."

I turned my attention to the prairie before us and rested my head against his shoulder.

The land, bathed in moonlight, glowed with fat droplets of morning dew.

Ah, to share this view with him…what a gift.

The bugler's horn sounded to wake the camp.

I lifted my head and looked at Henry.

"It's only now four?"

"Josiah owed me a few minutes."

"And you spent them with me," I added, touched.

"I'd like to spend every minute with you. That scares me."

The frankness in his words and in his gaze scared me a little, too.

"Why?" I whispered.

"Ma had a plan for me, and I was content to go along with it: get an education, find a bride, marry, start a family, and work an elegant job in the city for the rest of my life. When Pa's friend Tobias von Sharp, a German immigrant Pa met on the docks in Philadelphia, devised a plan to settle out west, we all thought he'd lost his mind. He wrote, inviting Ma and Pa to join him in *God's country*. That letter lit a fire of wanderlust in both of 'em. My sedate, settled, society-minded folks suddenly couldn't sit still. They devoured news articles and stories about life on the prairie. I'm not sure they didn't make up their minds to go find Tobias the second his letter arrived.

"Within a few months, they'd sold most everything they owned and laid out their trip to Green Hills…almost the same route you're taking now."

"*We* are taking," I corrected.

"Yes, *we*," he conceded.

"*We* scare you?"

"Not *you*. Quite the opposite. *You* feel like…well, home. Or how I think home ought to feel."

My heart hammered in my chest. Henry's words — so open and honest — came awful close to a declaration of love. My spirit soared with hope.

"Tobias told Pa to bring a starter herd of cattle. I knew little of cows, but I could ride a horse as if I'd grown up on the plains. Years earlier, I bought Scout as a colt; rode him every day, even in the city. Confident Scout and I could wrangle cattle, I hired a few experienced cowboys to help me and set out for the markets in Kansas City. One week under the stars, listening to the cows moo and bellow in the field, and riding Scout for hours a day shook up my plans. After that first drive, I couldn't go back."

"You've been working as a drover ever since?"

"I have," Henry said with a smile that hinted at a tug of war going on inside his head, or maybe his heart. "Mostly driving cattle to and from Wichita, St. Louis, and Denver for Pa and Tobias, but I've got a herd of my own on a few acres in Green Hills. I've also worked on a crew for a huge outfit in Texas, another in Wyoming, and one in Montana."

"My goodness...Kansas, Missouri, Colorado, Texas, Wyoming, Montana—"

"Arkansas and Oklahoma," he added, teasing me with a nudge. "Don't forget those; they've become very important here recently."

I smiled at his sweet flirting, but it soon faltered as my mind reviewed the facts.

"I can see how being tied down to one place can't compare with the travels and the places you're used to."

"It'd be different, that's for sure," Henry agreed. "But *different* doesn't mean *bad*. It just means..."

"A change," I said, filling in the word I thought he'd wanted.

"Yeah," he said with finality. He studied me for a long moment, his eyes darting from mine to my lips and then back over my features to stare into my soul. "We'd better get back. Mr. Rawes'll be pushing everyone to leave as soon as possible after losing a day of travel and struggling through so few miles yesterday."

We talked little on the walk to camp, both of us pensive and subdued. But when we approached the campgrounds, Henry kissed the back of my hand and promised to meet me for breakfast, just as he had before.

I'd almost told him I love him. Sitting on the top of the world, safe in his arms, I'd wanted to share every bit of my heart. But I couldn't. I *wouldn't*...not when the weight of knowing might obligate Henry to abandon the life he craved and enjoyed.

Keeping the truth to myself didn't make it less...true.

And the truth was, I loved Henry Davis.

12

"He Could Be the One"
Song by Hannah Montana (2009)

Day 9 ~ April 28, 1883

The revelation hummed under my skin for two straight days.

On the first, I'd seen Henry at our normal times. We'd shared meals, played with the children, and snuck in a couple of snuggles.

On the second day, he'd been away from camp both before and after travel hours. Families were retiring from the campfire, and I'd all but given up on seeing him when I heard Henry's unique whistle.

It sounded like a warbler, but deeper and fuzzier than the delicate, metallic tone of the sweet yellow birds. No one else seemed to notice it.

I waved goodnight to my friends and ducked between two wagons. Confident Henry would find me, I entered the clearing beyond camp.

"Hi," he said, stepping from behind a tree.

"Hi," I answered.

"Sorry I didn't make it to supper."

"Have you eaten anything? I can put together a plate for you," I said, reaching for his hand to drag him back to my wagon.

"No…I'm okay," Henry said, sounding exhausted and far from okay. He glanced at our clasped hands and then looked into my eyes. His gaze moved over my face, as though absorbing my features. "I just needed to see you."

Closing the space between us, I wrapped him in a hug and buried my head into his chest. Henry's arms came around me, and his body relaxed with a deep exhale.

"Are you sure you're okay?"

"Every day on a wagon trail — or on a cattle drive — is long. They push a person to the limits of their abilities, show what one's made of. Today, one man tried giving up."

"Giving up?" I echoed. "What does that mean? We can't *give up* out here. We're in the middle of nowhere. What did he think to do?"

Henry didn't answer; he just held me. Then I understood.

"He wanted to end his life," I whispered. "Oh, Henry."

His arms tightened, and he dropped his forehead against my hair.

"You said he tried to give up. Someone found him in time?"

"Yes, we found him in time."

"He's one of your drovers?"

"No," Henry whispered. "A man on the wagon train."

My head lifted from his chest to look into his face.

"A husband? A father?" I couldn't comprehend the enormity of such a situation. "He wanted to abandon his family to travel this road alone? To drive a wagon and a team of oxen across thousands of miles? Without him?" My heart broke for his wife, for his kids. And as mad as I was at the unknown man, my heart broke for him, too. How lost he must be, how smothered in fear he must feel. Releasing my ire, I settled back into the place where I fit so perfectly, sheltered in the sturdy frame of Henry's strength. "Thank God you got there in time."

"Mr. Moody and Doc Abbott are there now, and we've been taking turns driving his wagon and sitting with him. Just making sure he's not alone, that he knows he's got help and that we'll see him through."

"All that on top of driving the cows, seeing to their health and safety, and watching over the camp at night."

"Don't forget courting a beautiful woman I met on the trail."

"Are you now?" I teased, grinning up at him.

"I sure hope so," Henry said, surveying my response in earnest.

My grin blossomed into a huge smile.

"We better get you back to camp," he said, tucking my hand into the crook of his arm…funny how we'd already established our habits and norms. I liked that one — the way we leaned into one another while we walked — very much.

"Will I see you in the morning?" It was his night to watch over us.

"Not until breakfast. Phoebe, you need to stay in the circle, especially at night. Please?"

"Are we in danger?"

"We still don't know who's following us. Josiah took a couple of guys with him to backtrack and find them, but until we figure out who it is and why they're out there, I don't want to take any chances. Not with you. Tell me you'll stay put… that you'll stay with the group."

"I will," I promised. "You'll find me waiting for you under a shade tree with a heaping plate of bacon and eggs and biscuits and gravy and—"

"You're making me hungry," he laughed, scooping me up with a twirl before setting my feet back on the ground.

"Just trying to make sure you know what you'll be missing if you're tempted to sleep through church."

"That's not a bad thought," Henry joked. His teasing turned into a dramatic grunt when I playfully elbowed his ribs. About twenty yards from our wagon, he stopped in front of me. "Nothing will ever stop me from coming to you, at least nothing I can control," he said, all traces of humor gone. "*Nothing*," he repeated.

Then he kissed my hands and disappeared into the dark cover of the night.

I floated through my nighttime ablutions.

I hummed a merry tune while setting out my bedding.

Then I slept like a baby, without a single nightmare.

All I did was dream. *My, oh, my, what lovely dreams.*

Day 10 ~ April 29, 1883

*"M*iss Phoebe," Henry said, dropping his chin to greet me at breakfast. His eyes never left mine. A subtle smile played at the corner of his mouth, as though we shared a secret.

More than one, it seemed.

He'd seen me swimming in the Arkansas River our first morning on the trail. That should still embarrass me: him seeing me in only my nightclothes, witnessing my flagrant display of pain. It had. I was horrified when he revealed the viewpoint from the guard post. But not anymore. Knowing he'd seen me at such a state, viewed the most raw and most real me, no longer bothered me in the least.

Perhaps the timing made a difference. Henry'd stumbled upon my outburst our second morning on the trail. That night, when he'd shown me the lookout spot, we'd hardly known one another. Since then, we'd shared so much…our meals, our thoughts, and even our hearts.

I returned Henry's smile, admiring the playful confidence in his expression.

Many times, Henry stepped in to repair a wagon or coax headstrong oxen without making a show that might've brought shame upon the man unable to do the job on his own. On the morning we met, he'd suggested a modification to the wagon master's route for the day in a way that didn't second-guess the man's expertise or his authority. When rowdy boys' rambunctious play progressed too far, Henry administered correction with a tone that brooked no argument yet conveyed patience and understanding.

He would've been one of those energetic youngsters, champing at the bit to run wild with friends, resisting boundary lines set in place for his safety, and unable to resist the temptation of wide-open spaces in this stunning terrain.

The vision of his childhood morphed into the man studying me.

My lips, chapped from windy days spent walking with the children, chose that moment to burn and tingle like fire consumed the tender flesh. I moistened them, pulling one corner of my bottom lip between my teeth. Mortified by how coquettish I must've appeared, I dropped my gaze to the ground in self-recrimination. Thank the heavens Mama wasn't around to scold me, for she'd have been right to do so!

Henry monopolized my line of sight. He stood with his

boots rooted to the ground as though he'd happily remain right there, frozen in time *with me*, for eternity.

Before finding me at breakfast, Henry must've walked to the river to rinse his face with fresh water because droplets clung to his short brown hair and reflected the light. The effect reminded me of a kaleidoscope I once saw, the dazzling patterns so vivid I couldn't put it down.

Henry was just as beautiful.

My perusal didn't seem to offend him.

Still wearing a pleased expression, he watched me as my gaze flowed over his frame from toe to head. He assessed me as I studied him.

When I cleared my throat to speak, his chin tilted. He seemed to hang on my every word.

He could be the one.

13

***...I myself, will risk everything
rather than harm should reach you.
The Pathfinder, Chapter VIII
by James Fenimore Cooper (1840)***

*H*e could be the one. The thought filtered through my mind as second time, as though the Lord whispered the words only for me.

"You must be starving," I stated, a brilliant conversationalist to be sure.

"I am that," Henry answered, parched as well if one judged by the gravelly sound of his voice.

"This is for you," I said, offering the plate I'd just filled.

His eyes expanded at the amount of breakfast I'd piled on the plate.

"You'll have to help me," he said, knowing full well I was just about to go through the line to make my own plate.

A challenge gleamed in his eyes.

He'd effectively tossed a gauntlet at my feet.

We'd shared many meals together since Henry joined the wagon train, spent many evenings together around the fire. In silent agreement, we'd varied where we sat and with whom we dined and sang and danced, but people noticed. Mama had to realize how much time Henry and I spent together.

As much as I dreaded another showdown with Mama, I couldn't tolerate the notion of saying no.

I'd prayed for someone that electrified my senses and consumed my thoughts. In Boston, I watched friends and neighborhood girls become betrothed and get married. I'd memorized and revisited Jeremiah 29:11. *For I know the thoughts that I think toward you, says the LORD, thoughts of peace and not of evil, to give you a future and a hope.*

Twirling my skirts with sass and casting Henry a *follow me* look over my shoulder, I turned to set my empty plate back on the stack.

"Never eaten like this on the trail," the wagon master said with an air of condemnation rather than gratitude as he glared at the food I'd helped prepare. He didn't seem to be speaking to me, but I didn't feel as though I could walk away after hearing such a comment.

Known for scouting the families' offerings and choosing what looked most appealing on a meal-by-meal basis, he'd become a staple at the Williamson-Wilson-Barrett table. "Where'd them peaches come from? Fancy jam! I've never… Seems like foolish luxuries. No need for them in camp," he scoffed. While complaining, he'd piled seven peach halves on his plate alongside two scoops of butter and a heaping spoonful of jam on *each* of his three yeast rolls.

Henry flashed a quick, reassuring wink at me.

"You're right, Mr. Rawes," I replied in my most ardent attempt at gentle refinement, truly a performance to make

Mama proud. "I'd just canned those peaches — my grand-mother's recipe, no less — the week before our train departed for Van Buren. The thought of throwing them out was more than I could bear. It was quite silly, I now realize, to hope they'd be a treat to enjoy out here on the trail. The sooner we get through them, the better. It's the best way to lighten our wagon load, so you eat as many as you'd like."

The wagon master garbled a response…something better left indeterminable, I imagined. He also helped himself to two more spiced peach halves.

"Stunning *and* cunning," Henry whispered, close to my ear, so only I could hear. Warm air from his breath heated my nape while his compliment bolstered my spirit.

Certain my cheeks blushed bright pink, I walked away from the gathered crowd to sit on my quilt. I'd laid it out under the thick canopy of a splendid red maple, which looked dignified and majestic in a copse of trees growing in the open space of our wagon circle.

I glanced over my shoulder to find Henry following on my heels. Within a few steps, he'd splayed a hand on the small of my back…staking claim. When we reached my quilt, he held my hand to help me sit…staking claim. And when he sat beside me, he sat very close, with his body angled my way. His posture, protective and possessive, left no doubt that I was the object of his attention — all his attention. Anyone watching would assume us married, or betrothed at the least.

Henry *was* staking his claim. On me. By announcing his intentions. One could not interpret such a public display in any other way.

He likes me. A lot.

"Eat," he said with a knowing grin. "You said you'd help me with the feast you created on this plate."

Speechless and absent-minded, I picked at dried fruit. He

spread butter and jam on a biscuit and put it in my hand. I picked at that, too. When I'd finished nibbling the bread, he passed me a slice of bacon.

Henry attacked the food with much more vigor. Who knew when he'd last eaten. Within ten minutes, he'd cleaned the plate.

"I'll take that to the wash table," I offered, still in a stupor. Mama would be furious. It was one thing to sit with and converse with a gentleman at a meal. She'd even allowed dancing at parties and strolls in the park. She didn't hide her displeasure at Henry's presence with the children in the afternoons, but she'd not made too much of a fuss. But *this* — Henry's blatant familiarity…in the middle of the campgrounds…on a Sunday morning when everyone would notice — would most certainly incite her wrath.

"I've got it," Henry said, taking the uneaten bacon from my hand. He placed it on the plate, grinned *and winked* at me, and said, "I'll be right back." His low, yet firm voice lent assurance, a promise that we were indeed a *we*, that I'd not face Mama's anger alone, that he would, in fact, always be back.

My nerves abated and my head cleared.

Henry returned with two steaming mugs, one with coffee for himself and one with hot water for me. He surprised me by sliding a sachet of tea into my palm as he handed over my metal mug, carefully so the water didn't slosh over the rim. "Your favorite, I believe," he said, prompting me to look closer at the tea with his nod toward my hand.

I set the mug down and lifted my hand to smell the tea. Cinnamon, orange, and clove… "How did you know?" I marveled. "Where did you find this?"

"I'd like to take the credit for the elation on your face right now, but I had help," Henry said, shrugging as he confessed. "Back at the jumping off camp, my cousin Julianna mentioned a lovely young woman traveling with the train had enjoyed her homemade blend of spices, dried fruit, and black tea. I bartered to bring you all she had on hand."

"You were at the staging inn? In Van Buren?"

"Yes, I arrived the same night as you, but there weren't enough rooms, so Josiah and I slept in the barn."

"You're related to the innkeeper?"

"Yes, that's why Pa's instructions to your ma put you with a wagon train starting from there instead of Independence or Fort Smith. Julianna and Josiah are siblings," Henry filled in for me. "We grew up together. Josiah and I are close to the same age and more like brothers than cousins."

"He's your best friend."

Henry nodded. "In addition to mentor, confidant, and comrade-in-arms," he added, his eyes alight with deep respect and devotion.

"Who's older?"

"Josiah, by almost three years."

"Is he angry you're here, sharing another meal with me instead of doing drover things with the other cowboys?"

"No." Henry answered without hesitation. "Josiah's still out with the scouting party, investigating our followers. I hope he makes it back to camp this morning. If not, I'll ride out after church to see if I can help."

"Are you concerned that he's not back already?"

"They've been gone longer than we expected."

"I'll pack food for you to take…if you have to go. They likely didn't take many provisions if they'd planned to be back sooner."

"You don't have to do that."

"I want to," I said to assure him. "I'll pack a jar of spiced peaches…while they last," I added with a grin.

Henry chuckled.

"Poor Mr. Rawes has no clue he received a good, old-fashioned dressing-down," he said, shaking his head.

"I don't know what you're talking about," I said, feigning an innocent tone.

"You were masterful."

I waved off his praise. "I learned from the best... Mama's something to behold. I have a lot of fun watching her rule the world with an iron fist. Even when I'm the subject of her ire, she's exceptional. I see the love behind her actions...not everyone from our neighborhood did, back in Boston. Papa did, though. They loved one another so completely. He taught me to see her gifts. She never waivers in her convictions, and she doesn't suffer fools," I said with pride. "Her victims say *thank you* after she kills them with kindness."

"I can imagine," Henry allowed.

"And you've been warned."

"*Touché*," Henry said quietly. He studied my face, earnest with concern. Mr. Moody shuffled toward the rock he'd chosen as his pulpit, and Mrs. Moody passed out another song she'd chosen to share with the camp: "Blessed Assurance."

We sang several hymns, and Mr. Moody taught a lesson on Hebrews 10:22. *Let us draw near with a true heart in full assurance of faith, having our hearts sprinkled from an evil conscience, and our bodies washed with pure water.*

Josiah did not make an appearance; I sensed Henry's unease.

He'd want to ride out instead of visit with others after the church service.

While Henry returned our mugs to be washed, I gathered my quilt from the ground.

Before I could even shake off the dirt and leaves, Henry returned. He took two corners of the quilt from my hands, slowly, so our fingers brushed. Without words, we removed the debris and then folded the ends together, in a manner that brought us face-to-face with every fold. Once tidied, Henry draped the heavy fabric over his arm and faced me, his back to the crowd to create a scrap of privacy.

His eyes never left mine. I couldn't have looked away if a cannon boomed.

"You're Jasper," I stated, daring Henry to admit he'd been the one to leave the book with my belongings on my quilt. I'd figured it out days earlier. We'd been chatting about authors and books we'd loved as children. Every title Henry mentioned centered around exploration and adventure. When he told me about his upbringing in Philadelphia, when he talked about attending college and reading law, and when we discussed settlers facing tough decisions about keeping only those possessions that mean the most when moving out west…well, I'd just known in my heart that the beautiful books had to be Henry's.

"Perhaps in that I would willingly lose my life to carry you home safely."

The directness of his steel-gray eyes left no doubt of his sincerity. Henry's serious demeanor, normally so warm and amiable, held my attention. Like the red-tailed hawk's powerful wings beating the wind, a flutter started in my chest and pushed a humming vibration through my limbs before settling in my stomach.

Meeting his gaze with my chin held high, I willed my eyes to express what society deemed improper to say aloud. *I see you. I trust you. I believe in you.*

"You share many traits with both Jasper Western and the pathfinder. All three of you possess noble character, resourcefulness, and skill. You choose to live with honor, putting innate intelligence to good use."

"Not sure about all that," Henry said, dodging my admiration. "We can agree on one thing, though." His eyes darted to scan the surrounding area as people wandered toward their wagons and campfires. "They both recognized a precious treasure…" Henry ran the back of his fingers down my cheek. He brushed his thumb over my aching bottom lip and lifted my chin with gentle firmness until my eyes bore into his. "…and so do I."

His eyes shifted from mine, surveying the shadows the grove of trees created. My eyes closed.

And then he kissed me.

14

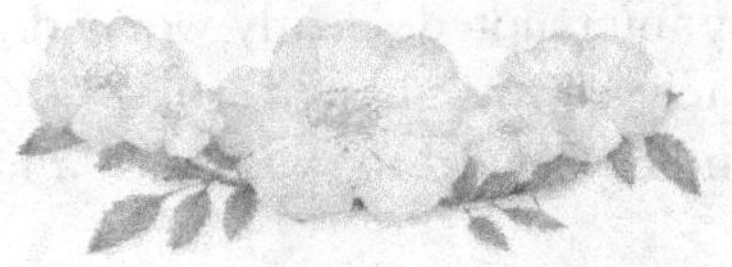

"Then He Kissed Me"
Song written by Phil Spector,
Ellie Greenwich, and Jeff Barry
Recorded by The Crystals (1963)

Having never been kissed before that delectable moment under my now favorite tree in the whole wide world, I couldn't say if fireworks *always* go off while kissing.

But I'd like to find out.

I wanted to find out immediately, with a second kiss from Henry. Maybe a third.

For the first time in my life, I understood the term *swoon.*

I sighed a dreamy sigh. The passion I'd sensed straining behind his control thrilled me. The whole encounter nearly overwhelmed me.

Had his arm around my torso not been supporting my wobbly legs, I'm certain I would have swooned my way straight to the ground.

Granting permission and making my wishes known, I

raised my chin. Lifting my lips toward Henry's, I angled for that second kiss.

It wasn't to be… Charlie approached, and Henry stepped aside to speak with him quietly.

"They never came back. I need to go," he said when he turned back to me.

"I'll gather provisions for—"

"No," Henry interrupted, clearly worried. "No, thank you. Save a jar of peaches for us, though…okay?"

I nodded, finding it hard to speak past a lump that formed in my throat.

Henry cupped the back of my neck and leaned down to place a warm kiss on my forehead.

"Be safe," I called as he walked away.

Day 11 ~ April 30, 1883

*H*enry didn't show up the rest of that day or the next.

I'd replayed our kiss a thousand times in my head. My lips felt different, changed. They tingled when I remembered the pressure of his mouth on mine. They yearned for his touch.

Absently, I ran my fingers over them, trying to soothe them.

I felt his absence in my heart as well. It ached for him. Working throughout the day, I thought of a million things I wanted to tell him. I kept one ear tuned to the ground, desperate to hear his voice.

I hadn't heard Mama's voice all day, either. She'd given me the silent treatment since church. *Don't let it bother you,* Papa would've said. *She'll come around… Silence is her way of working through things.*

But it did bother me.

My relationship with Papa was unique…precious; I'd shared everything with him, and he'd been my biggest fan… the glitter sparkling in my world. Mama's personality differed from his, more like glue that fused our family together…strong and immovable. She and I didn't gush over fabrics and fashion together as some of my school friends did with their mothers, but we'd always shared a camaraderie and a mutual, allied understanding. I feared losing that bond.

Anxiety over both Henry and Mama knotted my stomach.

*B*y that evening, I resembled a steam engine about to blow.

I couldn't sit still. I couldn't read, and I couldn't put the brakes on my wild imagination. I envisioned Henry hurt, Mama hating me, and my life ruined.

Quilting didn't help. Reading didn't help. Pacing in circles next to our wagon didn't help.

The longer I tried to think of something — *anything* — else, the worse it became.

Determined to distract my derailed train of thoughts, I decided to make a blend of oatmeal to have ready for the morning. Opening the hatch of our chuck box, I gathered rolled oats, raisins, dried apples and peaches, cinnamon, sugar, and pecans. When Mama refused to acknowledge a question I'd asked about empty jars, I came unglued.

"Yell, scream, curse if you need to," I told her. "Tell me you're mad, that I embarrass you. Lecture me about sending the right message and maintaining proper decorum. Review the dictates of manners and etiquette until we're both blue in the face. Just say *something* to me."

"There is no point in theatrics," she spat through tight lips. "A lady does not lower herself to flagrant language as a means of communication. I choose *not* to adopt the plebeian practices of common folks just because we've left polite society."

"*Common folks?* You think them low-class," I declared. "You believe the families with which we travel — side-by-side, dusty hour after dusty hour — are beneath you."

She reverted to ignoring me.

"Ha," I spouted. "Those commoners are doctors and lawyers and aristocrats, as well as farmers and ranchers, teachers and preachers, and even down on their luck shop-keepers."

That fanned a flame in her eyes.

"You interpret my time with the children as degrading? Well, I see it as a service. *Do not withhold good from those to whom it is due, when it is in the power of your hand to do so.* Proverbs 3:27… *Look not every man on his own things, but every man also on the things of others.* Philippians 2:4… *But to do good and to communicate forget not: for with such sacrifices God is well pleased.* Hebrews 13:16… Shall I go on? Didn't Jesus, himself, provide an example of a servant-hearted friend for us to follow?"

She didn't answer, so I kept going.

"My feelings for Henry disgust you? Well, I love him. I do! It's all-consuming, and it's beautiful, and it's good."

Still, she remained frozen as stone.

"*And though I have the gift of prophecy, and understand all mysteries and all knowledge, and though I have all faith, so that I could remove mountains, but have not love, I am nothing,*" I began. "1 Corinthians 13:2… *But above all these things put on love, which is the bond of perfection.* Colossians 3:14… *And the LORD God said, It is not good that the man should be alone; I will make him an help meet for him.* Genesis 2:18. Mama, I am meant for Henry, and he is meant for me."

"You will not marry that man." The vehemence in her voice shocked and saddened me.

"If he asks, I will."

"To do *what?* Ride along on cattle drives?" she scoffed. "Live *where?*"

"I'll go wherever Henry leads. Being together is what matters."

"Grow up, Phoebe," she said, dismissing my feelings with disdain.

"I have, Mama. So has my heart."

"Time will tell," she said, her tone an accusation, as though she hoped for the worse instead of my happiness.

"What is that supposed to mean?"

"It means plans are already in motion, plans for your future…the future your father and I intended for you."

She didn't raise her voice…showed no emotions. Her icy, calm demeanor scared me.

"Excuse me." Henry's voice caught my attention. So engrossed in the argument with Mama, I'd not seen him approach. The oppressive atmosphere around me lifted at the sight of him. Then I registered his pallor, pale and ashen. His eyes appeared hollow, the silver sparkle I adored in them missing. His jaw ticked. Something was wrong.

I moved toward him. Henry stepped back.

"Ladies, I apologize for interrupting." Why so cold and formal? I held his gaze for another moment, begging for answers. Then he turned to Mama. "Your company is here, ma'am."

"Her what?" I clamored.

Henry only nodded in our general vicinity, turned on his heels, and walked away.

*A*nother man, who'd been standing behind Henry, took his place.

"Mrs. Williamson…Miss Williamson," he said. "Lieutenant

Commander Xavier Holland, pleased to make your acquaintance." The man clipped his heels together with a half-bow. Tall and lean with jet black hair, he wore a crisp, blue naval uniform. Gold trim, running down the outside of each pant leg, and gold buttons, spaced with precision from collar to belt looked out of place in the middle of Indian Territory and so far from his duties.

"Phoebe," Mama instructed. "Meet your betrothed."

My eyes ricocheted from Mama to the stranger and back again.

I looked in the direction where Henry had disappeared.

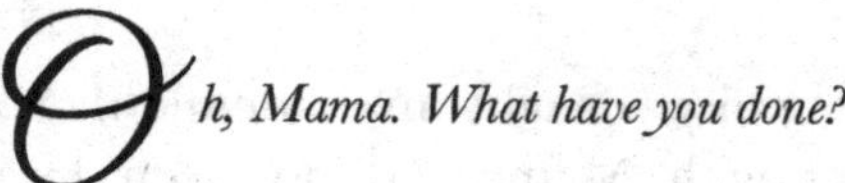

Oh, Mama. What have you done?

15

*When a gentleman has become fascinated
by a fair lady whom he is most anxious to know more
particularly, we venture to give him a word of serious
advice. We urge him to consider well his position and
prospects in life, and reflect whether they are such as
to justify him in deliberately seeking to win the young
lady's affections, with the view of making her his wife
at no distant period.*

"First Steps in Courtship"
Collier's Cyclopedia of Commercial
and Social Information
and Treasury of Useful and
Entertaining Knowledge,
Compiled by P.F. Collier (1883)

"Mr. Holland—"

"Lieutenant Commander," he corrected.

"Excuse me?" I asked, befuddled by his interruption.

"My correct title is Lieutenant Commander Holland. I've

come to fulfill my obligation of marriage to Miss—" He paused, retrieving a folded packet of papers from a smaller, less militant-looking man positioned exactly three feet behind and to the left of himself. Mr. Holland consulted the document before continuing. "—Phoebe Victoria Williamson. She is you?"

I stared at him as though he'd grown a second head.

"You are her?" he tried again.

I'd fallen into a science fiction novel like the Jules Verne's stories Papa had enjoyed, even though they existed in alternate realities. That had to be it…because in the real world, *Henry* and I were betrothed. I couldn't be engaged to Lieutenant Commander Whoever; I loved Henry.

I love Henry!

And Henry loved me — I was sure of it.

I just needed to make sure he was, too.

Henry. I have to find Henry.

I twirled to flee in the direction he'd gone, but Mama stopped me in my tracks.

"This is Victoria," she said with the utmost grace. "Your bride-to-be. The sooner the wedding, the better. I'll go for the preacher."

*A*gain, I wasn't a person to throw tantrums. Nor was I a girl who fainted.

Until I hit the wagon trail.

Day 12 ~ May 1, 1883 ~ after midnight

Some unknown amount of time after Mama's unfathomable declaration, I awoke surrounded by Mrs. Moody, Mrs. Wilson, Margaret, Mrs. Barrett, and a few additional women whose names I couldn't grasp through the fog in my head.

I remembered hearing Mama say something that included the words *bride, wedding,* and *preacher.* I'd glanced over my shoulder at her, sure I misunderstood. Then a ringing started filling my ears and darkness encroached on my peripheral vision until the entire world turned black.

"Oh, Phoebe," Margaret gasped upon noticing my eyes open. "Are you okay?"

"No," I said, panic seizing my lungs once again.

Mrs. Wilson eased me back when I tried sitting up.

"Give it a minute, dear," she crooned, fussing about me like a nursemaid. "You had quite a fall."

"A fall?" I wondered, beyond confused. Maybe the naval officer had been a bad dream.

I watched Mrs. Moody pray over me while Mrs. Wilson fetched a glass of water. I viewed the scene as a spectator, floating around the activity but not part of it…until Mrs. Barrett dabbed at my forehead with a tincture that set my skin on fire.

That cleared the cobwebs.

"Margaret, find Henry," I instructed, trying — and failing — to push the team of women away so I could go find him myself. "I need Henry!"

My forceful demand got everyone's attention. They froze to gape at me.

"I'm here," his firm voice answered from behind the wall of busybodies.

They split like the Red Sea, and yes, there he was.

The invisible weight on my chest vanished like a mist.

Ahhh, better.

"I had the most horrible dream," I said, reaching for him as he walked nearer. "Mama refused to accept that I'm not interested in *any* husband. In my nightmare, she'd sent for some stranger to force me to wed. It was awful. I couldn't marry that man. She knows I'm holding out for a husband who's also a friend, someone who looks at me as Papa looked at her. I—"

I'm looking for love, I was going to say.

The look on Henry's face stopped me.

He'd crouched beside the bed, which was really a door often used as a table that someone had covered in quilts. But he'd not held my hands.

I reached for him, clawing at the air until he grasped my fingers. He did not entwine them with his as he should've.

"You've blood on your shirt," I said, hyper focused on the red stain coloring his neck and collar.

"It's from the cut on your head, Miss Williamson."

"Don't call me that," I said, angry and hurt.

"I'm sorry," he said, his eyes full of agony. He brought his lips to the back of my hands before stacking them on the bedding as he stood and walked away.

"Henry," I called out. "Henry!" I yelled, but my voice broke.

He must not have heard because he didn't turn back.

I wanted to go after him, to— I don't know what, but I needed him.

Every time I tried to escape, a different woman stepped in to block my way, nudge me to lie down, beg me to stop fighting.

Dr. Abbott arrived, threatening to give me laudanum if I didn't calm down to rest.

"You fainted, Miss Williamson," he said in a patronizing tone. "Your head hit a rock on the ground and gashed your temple. You received seven stitches, which you're going to tear if you don't settle. Either you rest by choice or by medication; which will it be?"

That had done the trick; I hated medications and would do almost anything to avoid laudanum. I stilled immediately.

"That's more like it," Dr. Abbott said with a smile and his usual voice.

"I—"

He raised a hand to stop me.

"Hold that thought, please," he said. "Ladies? Thank you for your assistance; you've each been invaluable. Now Miss Williamson needs some space and quiet. Let's let her rest until morning, shall we?"

He pretended to jot notes in a small leather journal while the women stalled, searched for reasons to stay, and slowly left the canvas-covered medical area that Dr. Abbott set up beside his wagon every evening.

Once the last person had walked far enough to be out of earshot, he slid the book into his coat pocket and sat on a log next to me.

"Now then," he began. "Let's talk."

"I need Henry," I said, getting right to the point.

Dr. Abbott grinned. "He needs you, too."

"But he left," I argued. "I don't understand."

"Emotions are high right now. Things will work themselves out. Have faith in that. But they won't get sorted right now. Above all, you need rest — I wasn't just saying that to chase away the nurse brigade," he said with a knowing smile.

"What happened?"

"Let's just say you missed the fireworks."

"But—"

Again, he lifted a hand to interrupt. Then he filled a mug from a pot warming over a small fire. "Sip this broth, and I'll fill you in…but *only* if you promise to stay put."

"Deal," I promised, reaching for the broth. I inhaled the steam rising from the mug; my stomach responded to the aroma of chicken broth seasoned with herbs and vegetables with a loud growl.

"That's a good sign," Dr. Abbott said with a silent laugh.

"What time is it?"

"Just after two in the morning," he answered after consulting his pocket watch.

"Henry should've been on duty; it was his night to guard the camp."

"He stayed right by your side— well, as much as he could with so many anxious volunteers seeing to your recovery." He shook his head with a smile.

"They mean well," I said. "But are a lot to take *en masse*," I added, which turned his smile into a laugh.

"True," he agreed. "Miss Wilson stayed calm and patient. She'd make an excellent nurse, if someone wanted to hint at it with a gentle nudge."

"Margaret has a sweet nature and a kind heart. She's also a quick study. I'll see what I can do to plant a seed."

"She handled seeing your blood considerably better than did poor Henry."

"Henry? *My* cowboy?" I couldn't believe that. Henry cleaned fish, tended livestock, and killed deer, snakes, squirrels, chickens, and even his cows when necessary.

Dr. Abbott lifted an eyebrow at my possessiveness, but I didn't care. I was Henry's, and Henry was mine…regardless of Mama and her mysterious groom.

"It's different when the blood belongs to someone you love," he said. A shadow darkened his eyes, but he shook it off. "Henry looked worse than you when he brought you to the tent. I wasn't sure whom to treat first," he teased.

"But Henry wasn't there when I fainted. Was he?" The details still eluded my memory.

"According to Miss Wilson, when you fainted face down, your mother thought it was a scheme. She pushed you over onto your back and let out quite a scream at the sight of your face — keep in mind head wounds bleed profusely. Henry must've been close by because he heard your mother's cry and came to your aid. He carried you in here and never left."

"Until I woke up," I said. "Perhaps I should've remained unconscious." I harrumphed with sulkiness.

"You wouldn't feel that way if you'd seen the stark fear in his face with your limp body in his arms."

I smirked at the good doctor. "Thank you," I drawled. "I feel sufficient loads of guilt for my petulance."

Dr. Abbott laughed. Smile lines appeared around his mouth and eyes, bringing attention to his friendly countenance. He didn't possess rugged good looks like Henry, but he was handsome, with the well-groomed, highly educated look of a doctor in New York or London or Paris. Tall and trim, deep green eyes, pleasant features…he likely had women falling at his feet, just as I supposed Henry did wherever he went.

"You're not an ogre," I said, since apparently we'd become friends who tease one another for fun. "I'm still alive, so you're not a quack doctor, either. Why isn't there a Mrs. Abbott in our wagon train?"

The shadows returned to his eyes, and I wished I could take back the innocent question.

"It's okay," I said in a hurry. "You don't need to answer that. Mama says I speak first and think last far too often. I apologize for prying."

"Some people are made for walks in Central Park and evenings at the Metropolitan Opera. They shimmer and shine, thriving in the constant thrum of society and charities and balls and gowns. Motion makes them happy. Art galleries and museums bring them joy…they keep the world moving forward because nothing stops them, not even the hands on a clock or the physics of time. Other people crave open spaces, quiet strolls under the stars, and early nights. Long days of doing — rather than going — provide a sense of accomplishment that fills an essential need in their souls. The seasons and the passing of time mark their days rather than the time on a clock face. Both groups of people are *right*, both deserve to live a fulfilling life. They just can't do it together."

"Mama's happiest in the first group. I worry about how she'll adjust to life in the country."

"And you?"

"Is it pathetic that I want only to be where Henry wants to go?" I didn't give him time to answer. "I enjoyed our life in Boston, the bustling energy of the city, the people and the scenery. But I love the scenery out here on the trail, too…the birds singing with the sunrise, the patience and perpetuity I see in nature…sitting with Henry each evening as the crystal blue sky transitions through an explosion of colors, the clouds glowing with fire before the sun disappears on the horizon. I think I can be happy anywhere, doing anything, as long as he's with me."

"That's lovely, not pathetic. And it's a gift, a rare one. Not everyone meets their soulmate on earth."

"I know," I said, nodding at the truth in what he said. "I can feel it, sense it somehow. What draws Henry and I together is special and unique. And it's worth fighting for," I said, more spirited than intended.

"He's fighting for you," Dr. Abbott said quietly.

"By walking away?"

"He's fighting for you," he said with assurance. "He's putting your happiness over his own. That's what true love does."

"That makes no sense to me," I argued. "My happiness is tied to his. To *him*."

"If he could only be happy — truly fulfilled — living the

life he's loved on the open range, nomadic and free, would you force him to give it up? For love?"

"Of course not," I said, too quickly perchance. "I would never ask nor expect that of Henry."

"So you'd give up your happiness for his?"

"You made your point," I said with a sigh. "Saying goodbye to Henry would crush me, but for him, I would."

"And he for you."

"But—" I argued, but Dr. Abbott continued over my objections.

"Officer Holland—" I scoffed at the title. "—offers an opportunity for you to return to the life you knew and enjoyed in the city. His rank comes with benefits and affluence, fortune and means well beyond what your family knew as successful shopkeepers."

"I neither want nor need those things," I said, lifting my chin in defiance.

Dr. Abbott refilled my mug of broth. He raised an eyebrow and tapped my nose twice, stuck up in the air like an ostentatious hot-air balloon.

Chastised again.

"Thank you," I said, grateful for the broth and the reprimand.

"It's not just you, though. Is it? A way back to the East Coast is an opportunity for your mother, too."

16

The deer that goes too often to the lick
meets the hunter at last!
The Pathfinder, Chapter VI
by James Fenimore Cooper (1840)

Dr. Abbott gave me a lot to think about. Then he ordered me to sleep.

Surprisingly, I did, right through the wake-up call, right through breakfast preparations, and almost through load-up.

"She's not strong enough to walk," I heard Dr. Abbott say from around his wagon.

"Good, then we will stay here until she is," Mama answered.

"I can't advise that, either, ma'am. It would be a substantial risk to your safety, staying on the trail without the security of the wagon train."

"Lieutenant Commander Holland will protect us," she boasted.

"The good doctor has a valid point, Mrs. Williamson," someone chimed in, presumably the lieutenant commander himself. "My men and I were less of a target in our travels overland to find you because we stayed in constant motion, weaving between towns and outposts. A wagon and supplies act as a beacon, not to mention two lovely females who attract a lot of attention in the wilderness. Perhaps we should continue the trek to the next town with the wagon train and determine our plan of action from there?"

I heard a *hmph* followed by skirts swishing.

Mama grunting is a terrible sign.

"Good morning," Dr. Abbott said when he entered the tent, although I remained burrowed under quilts feigning sleep.

"Are they gone?" I asked with a stage whisper.

"The coast is clear," he said with a chuckle. "The better question is, how do you feel?" He handed me a plate holding dried fruit, bacon, and a biscuit.

"My head aches," I told him. "But the world isn't fuzzy anymore."

"Good," he mumbled, poking and prodding around the stitches. Then he leaned back to study me more.

"Is my hair standing on end?"

"I'm trying to decide what to do with you," he said.

"Now that abandoning me here on the frontier is off the table?" I asked with a smirk.

"We can both thank the Lord for that," he said, raising a conspiratorial eyebrow. "Walking for eight hours, on the other hand, is *off* the table."

Not walking meant riding. The thought of bumping around in the back of a wagon turned my stomach. My face must've reflected my dread.

"Think you can ride a horse?"

"Is that my only alternative?"

He halfway shrugged.

"I can do it…if the horse is gentle. And slow. And strong." A definite lack of confidence weakened my claim.

"How about Scout?"

I jolted upright at the sound of Henry's voice, then grabbed my head with regret.

"*Easy,*" Dr. Abbott warned. "Or I'll put you in a wagon, after all."

"I'll take care of her," Henry said.

Dr. Abbott clapped Henry on the shoulder as he walked out of the tent…a tap of gratitude? Or commiseration?

"Hi," I said, a feeble opening, but I didn't know what to say.

Henry didn't answer, instead walking to my bedside and crouching next to it as he had done the night before. He raised a hand to my head, caressing the skin around my cut before cradling my cheek in his palm. Henry's other hand joined it, and far too slowly, he leaned forward until his lips touched mine.

The kiss was nothing like our first, and yet it was far sweeter.

When Henry tried to pull away, I wrapped my hands around his wrists and dragged him back to me.

My head spun, buzzing either from the head injury or from the passion of our kiss escalating. I might've winced, and Henry must've noticed… He ended our kiss but didn't move far.

I slid toward the edge of the platform, creating room for Henry to sit on the edge…determined to do whatever I could to keep him close.

"I tried to stay away," Henry said, his voice raw with emotion. "Just couldn't."

"*Don't* try that again," I said. "Please?" I tried to sound firm, but my voice broke, making my command more of a plea. "You scared me last night. Why did you leave?"

"He has a contract."

"What?"

"Holland has a marriage contract; he says your father signed it."

"I don't understand. Papa's been gone for months."

"I haven't seen it, but Holland claims it's legal and that his parents and your parents arranged it years ago."

"Surely that's not binding. They can't force me into marriage. Papa would never have wanted something like that…*never.*"

"Are you sure?"

"Of course I am. Papa wanted me to pursue my education. We spoke of my applying to Radcliffe, the new women's annex at Harvard, even planned which courses I should take."

"Then maybe he *did* arrange this as a backup in case something happened. And then it did."

"No," I said, shaking my head in denial.

"As Holland's wife, those plans are possible. It's a path to achieving all your dreams."

"Dreams change," I argued with a thread of anger.

Henry looked at me with doubt and defeat heavy in his eyes. I hated it.

"Papa would *not* have done this," I urged, falling back on my primary argument. "He loved Mama with all his heart and wanted that type of marriage for me, too. Papa would never have agreed to this. I know it."

"But your mother might have."

Just then, Dr. Abbott returned. Margaret was with him. Henry stood and stepped back from the bed.

"The wagons are almost loaded," Dr. Abbott said. "I need to tear down and load as well. Phoebe, we'll step away so Margaret can help you."

My eyes jumped to Henry. I didn't want him out of my sight, but I needed help getting to the stream and preparing for the day.

"I'll be right here," he promised, reading my mind.

*W*hen Margaret and I returned, the guys had stored Dr. Abbott's medical supplies, loaded the makeshift bed, and even folded the canvas tent.

"Are we ready?" I asked, striving to sound excited when, in reality, I was terrified. I'd only ever ridden a horse for a few minutes, in the middle of the night, wrapped in Henry's embrace. How would I stay on the horse for four straight hours and maintain some semblance of respectability?

"I'm willing to try this, but I'm not sold on it," Dr. Abbott told me. "You must let me know — *immediately* — if you experience any dizziness, nausea, or sharp pain aside from the underlying headache you already have."

I nodded my understanding.

"Questions?" he asked.

"Only one," I said. "Did my mother come to the tent last night?"

*Y*our mother might have.

Henry had said it with compassion, but his tone held a twinge of distaste.

Dr. Abbott confirmed my suspicions… Mama had been there long enough to learn I would live, but she'd not been back since.

"What are you thinking?" Henry asked.

We'd been riding half an hour, staying slightly ahead of the wagons to avoid the dust, but close enough to stay in sight and within reasonable distance to Dr. Abbott, just in case.

Because we were in front of the train, no one saw the way I slumped against Henry's chest or how his arms held me in place. Scout's slow walk minimized my bouncing, and the ride was rather smooth.

"That I imagine you've never ridden this slowly in all your life," I answered, not wanting to talk about Mama. Or Xavier Holland. "Is it a problem that you're not with the cattle today?"

"I spend most of every day in this saddle, and I can't think of a time I've enjoyed it more," he replied. "And we did a little bartering to cover my shift driving the herd."

"We did?"

"Mm-hmm," Henry said. "We've agreed to bake one apple pie, two peach cobblers, and a batch of cowboy cookies."

"Is that all *we* need to make?"

"We also promised a couple of jars of jelly and a few mending favors."

"That's not too bad," I said, unable to contain my smile. "Sounds like *we* got off pretty easy."

"Well, I'm also cleaning noses every day until we arrive in Green Hills."

"Cleaning noses?"

"Like us, horses sweat, which lowers body temperature… helps us cool off after being on the trail all day. But oxen and cows don't. That makes 'em pant to cool off while we're traveling, but panting makes them inhale lots of dust. When dust coats their lungs, they can't breathe, which causes a whole host of additional problems."

"So, you clean their nostrils?"

"That's right."

"And you've been doing this every day we've been on the trail?" I asked.

"The cowboys share the load. The evenings I came to supper straight from the watering hole? Those were my days to clean noses."

"And now, because of me, you have to do it *every* day?"

"Not because of you," Henry said, his tone more serious. "For you."

"The guys would've covered my duties today without the bargain. I would've helped clean the oxen no matter what. The bargaining was just for fun…and to score some sweets," he teased. "But I figured you would've been happy to bake for 'em anyhow."

"I'm honored to," I said, meaning it with all my heart.

"And they're happy to help you."

"Us," I corrected.

"Us," he agreed.

"Is it too soon for there to be an *us?*" I asked, marveling at how easy, but quickly, we'd gotten to that point.

"If you'd asked me in Van Buren two weeks ago, I would've said yes. But after living the last twelve days with you on this trail, I can tell you I don't want to live any days without you. And that feels like the most natural thing in the world, like we're two puzzle pieces that fit together perfectly."

"We snapped right into place," I said.

"That we did," he agreed.

*W*hen we stopped for lunch, Henry warned that I might feel wobbly after being in the saddle for so long.

I protested that I needed to help put the meal together, but Dr. Abbott took Henry's side and forbade me from working just yet. They were right. I spent most of the hour trying to restore feeling in my legs so I could walk around a bit.

Mama ignored me from across the campground. Or maybe I avoided her. Either way, the imminent and difficult discussion ahead of us didn't happen. I was all too happy to put it off until Green Hills, but my luck ran out after supper that night.

Dr. Abbott didn't release me to do chores, but he allowed me to sleep at our wagon instead of the medical tent. I'd done well throughout the day, with no symptoms showing my head trauma had worsened. Other than the stitches and a bruised eye turning from red and puffy to black and blue, he'd determined I'd come through my ordeal unharmed.

I was preparing my bed under the wagon when Mama cornered me.

My first instinct was to look for Henry, but he'd said it would be a while before he returned from tending the livestock…cleaning noses, among other tasks.

"Have you considered the life ahead in Green Hills and compared it to the life waiting for you back east, possibly in Washington?" she said, jumping right over any pleasantries or concerns for my well-being.

"Washington?" I asked.

"Lieutenant Commander Holland——"

"Mama, do you really call him that every time you say his name?"

"Interrupting is rude and a sign of disrespect," she countered.

"My apologies," I said. "Please, continue."

Her lips pursed tighter. But she'd come to give a lecture, and I'd received enough of them over the years to know that once she'd prepared one, there was no stopping the delivery.

"Lieutenant Commander Holland has political aspirations. You can be a senator's wife, or even first lady."

"Mama, I don't want to be a society wife."

"You're always going on about educating people and making a difference. Phoebe, who do you think precipitates such advancements? The women behind the men, *that's who*," she said, pausing either for effect or to calm her agitation.

"I have thought a great deal about our new life in Green Hills," I said, addressing her initial question. "You know I'm not naive, and I know it won't be easy, certainly not luxurious. Everything I've read or heard about building a life in the West is that it's hard…*hard* to get set up, *hard* to thrive, and *hard* to survive."

"Then why do you still want to go when there's another option, a better option for a better life?"

"I'm not scared of the hard work. A new beginning excites me, and I'm eager to set up the new shop. I have so many ideas for the space and how we can serve the community as Green Hills continues to grow. They need us; they're counting on us. And we agreed to come, signed a contract. Don't you want to honor that commitment?"

"Are you scared of Indian attacks? Lawlessness? And as far as the documents with Green Hills, we have another contract that supersedes it."

I glowered in response.

"Would you like to see it?"

"Yes," I said, irritated by the way she lit up with hope so quickly. "But not until we get to Green Hills. Henry's father is an attorney. I'm not looking at anything without him present."

"Don't be ridiculous, Phoebe. This is a family matter."

"Mama, arranged marriages are an antiquated practice. Contracts are often overturned by a judge for lack of consent. You can't just marry me off, and you know Papa never would have allowed such a thing, either."

"Exactly when did you become a legal expert?"

"I'm not, but Henry is."

That set her back.

"That's right, Mama. Henry attended college in Pennsylvania and law school at Yale University in Connecticut. You dismissed him before you got to know him."

"Which is exactly what you're doing with Lieutenant—"

"*Don't* say it."

"It's true," she said, smirking. "You're too impulsive, Phoebe…have been since you were a toddler, roaring into the world without thinking through your actions. Are you really going to throw away a chance at a beautiful home and an elegant life, with resources and advantages most people can't imagine, to follow a cowboy on cattle drives, with little to no money, while living on a wagon trail, fighting dust and disease and starvation? Is he even going to marry you? Because so far on this trip, all he's done is ruin your reputation and make you look like a loose woman."

"Mama! We've done nothing wrong."

"Your actions speak for you, proving you've lost sight of who you are and *what* you are."

My will to fight deflated. Mama always won in the end. One way or another, she always struck the final blow.

"And *what*, Mama, do you think I am?" I asked, bracing for the impact.

"A sheltered young woman, lost after losing her father and making poor decisions in her grief…someone blessed to have the guidance and courage to set her path back on track…a debutante with the power to have it all."

17

"Oh Mama"
Song by Milky Chance (2019)

Day 13 ~ May 2, 1883

"Did you sleep?" I asked Henry, once we were ambling down the trail on Scout. Dr. Abbott had agreed to let me walk after nooning, if I rode the first part of the day.

The afternoon walk would be short, around two miles.

It was the day we would arrive in Green Hills.

"Some," Henry answered.

His arms held me in place. Our bodies shared warmth against a slight chill. Yet a distance existed between us I couldn't explain.

"I saw your boots," I confessed. "From my bedding under the wagon, I saw them…just beyond the wagon circle… watching over me."

It took Henry so long to reply, I thought he might say nothing at all.

"I dozed. Dragged a chair in the field. I needed to—"

His words faded, as if he didn't know how or didn't want to finish his thought.

"You don't have to explain," I said. "I just wanted to say thank you." I nestled into his chest — a reverse hug, I suppose, to close the gap between us.

Henry didn't say anything, but he relaxed a smidge, leaning into me as I did into him instead of sitting in the saddle like a stiff iron rod.

The silence worried me, but I wouldn't push. As Papa had said, some people prefer a quiet space to work through their thoughts… And we both had a lot on our minds.

Anticipation at seeing Green Hills with my own two eyes built with every passing minute. How would it look? How would it feel? Like home?

I didn't share Mama's opinions, but I had listened to what she'd said, considered the factors she'd asked me to think about. No doubt, her actions had been high-handed and manipulative. But they stemmed from worry and love.

She saw in me a woman shuffling through life under a blanket of grief, acting out of character, doing crazy things. I saw the same in her.

Mama lost her soulmate, her livelihood, and her home in a brief span of time.

That she'd kept moving forward was a testament to her strength.

Papa had managed the family finances and business affairs with meticulous accuracy and the strictest ethics. He didn't leave us destitute. In fact, we didn't owe a single grantor.

Nor did we own the building that housed both the store and our family.

Our landlord, Mr. Harden, refused to sell, and he refused to continue renting to two females, regardless of how important a role the shop played in our area of the city, just west of the Public Garden. Almost a hundred new homes were built in Back Bay, our thriving Boston neighborhood, over the past three years, and construction wasn't slowing down. Besides the beautiful homes and their unique elements of Parisian architecture, Back Bay attracted cultural institutions that constructed palaces dedicated to science, art, and religion — our Back Bay churches rivaled any in America. Despite the rapid growth, Back Bay did not, however, allow many businesses. Papa's mercantile, a jeweler, and a handful of upper-class boutiques were the only commercial entities in the area.

Within days of Papa's death, Mr. Harden went out of his way to sabotage our success. He vowed to destroy the structure to make room for a new home before he'd allow women to control business interests in Back Bay. We didn't dare call his bluff.

If Mr. Harden had allowed us to stay and continue running the store, we'd have never left Boston. I'd have been happy there, enjoyed a full life with all I wanted or needed. In time, I would've married, most likely to someone similar to Xavier Holland, and we'd have lived in Back Bay with other prominent and wealthy families. Not knowing any different, I would have loved that life.

But I would not have seen the plains, or the buffalo, or the sensational sunsets caused by prairies and fields of red dirt. I would not have met Henry.

Perhaps you were born for such a time as this.

The verse from Ruth waged a war between my heart and my head.

Everything Mama said made sense. If I were a mother— *When* I become a mother — I'll want the best life for my child, a life of peace and comfort, of happiness and good times. I won't want them in danger or strife. They'll need access to education and healthcare, a place to belong in the world that encourages betterment and philanthropy. I wouldn't find those things in a tiny burgeoning town in the middle of Indian Territory, surrounded by daily struggles. Survival took precedence over schooling, art galleries, and theater shows. The things on my list simply weren't in the West.

But Henry was, so there, too, was my heart.

And that — *he* — changed everything.

"Miss Phoebe, Miss Phoebe, Miss Phoebe," a band of hyper children called when I walked from where Henry tethered Scout to where the women prepared lunch and the children played.

Their hugs and exuberance provided the distraction I needed.

"Hello, my friends!"

"We missed you," Elise said, attaching herself to my arm. "Ma's baby still isn't here," she said with a defeated and grumpy sigh. I'd heard from the other ladies at nooning that Mrs. Jenkins's labor had begun, but Dr. Abbott hoped the baby would wait to appear until we'd arrived in Green Hills.

"But I hear he or she is on the way. And the baby quilt is ready to welcome the little one into the world when he or she decides it's time." I'd also heard Mrs. Jenkins wasn't doing as well as Dr. Abbott would've liked. She'd mentioned mild preeclampsia with Elise's birth, so Dr. Abbott monitored her blood pressure closely. He'd settled Mrs. Jenkins in his wagon and employed Margaret to keep her company, trying to keep Elise's mother calm and her contractions light for as long as possible.

"We're almost to Green Hills," Oliver pointed out. "That's your jumping off point. What about our story?"

"I think we can get through the final few chapters of Alice's adventure. And perhaps you'd like to select one or two of my books to take with you as the train continues on to Santa Fe. Would you like to read to the group after nooning each day?"

The child's love for literature and storytelling had blossomed in front of my eyes. He asked insightful questions about characters and plot. He liked to guess why every character said or did or thought every little thing. And he had a theory to answer each *why*. Every young boy dreamed of becoming Texas Jack or Wild Bill Hickok; Oliver was no different. But his thirst for adventure through words on a page increased with every day. I imagined his path leading to a career as a professor, or maybe even a writer…as long as books remained available to him. I'd speak to Louisa and Jude about it, encourage them to look for a library in Santa Fe. And if one didn't yet exist, I'd encourage them to advocate for the city to build one.

Before I formed you in the womb I knew you; Before you were born I sanctified you; I ordained you a prophet to the nations.

God had a plan for Oliver; I prayed it involved crossing my path again in the future. At the very least, I hoped to know where his journey would take him. I hoped to stay in touch with Louisa, Sarah, and Margaret, for sure, and hopefully Mrs. Moody and a few of the other women I'd befriended on the wagon trail.

Relative to a lifetime, the days with the wagon train were few. In terms of impact and experience, my time on the trail changed my life — changed *me*.

I detangled myself from the children to help with lunch.

Then we finished reading *Alice's Adventures in Wonderland*. Afterward, Oliver chose three books to keep, all stories I'd read multiple times…all with inscriptions from Papa that I'd hold in my heart forever, if not in my hands.

Once we'd finished loading the lunch supplies, the last stretch of my walk to Green Hills began.

I fought tears — of joy and uncertainty, some of anticipation and grief. Through the tightening of my throat, I led the children in singing all our favorite songs.

A valley of lush grasses, dense clumps of colorful flowers, and imposing green trees that formed picture-book canopies came into view as we topped a rise.

I lost my battle, letting my emotions roll down my cheeks with abandon.

I'd given the trip my all. Along the way, I discovered new friendships, learned new skills, and realized my strength. I found love.

Before me sat the culmination of that journey…my new home. It was bold and beautiful and held untold promises.

Welcome to Green Hills, the wind whispered in my ear.

"Why are you crying, Miss Phoebe? Are you sad?" Elise asked with a gentle tug on my hand.

"A little," I told her, wanting to be honest. "I'm sad to say goodbye to the families going on with the wagons tomorrow. But I'm also happy."

Trust in the Lord with all your heart, and lean not on your own understanding; In all your ways acknowledge Him, and He shall direct your paths.

"God brought me to Green Hills," I told the sweet girl. "I can't wait to see what He has planned for me here."

"What do you think He has planned for me?" Her little voice held threads of hope and fear.

"Big things," I said with a huge smile. "We can't fathom the dreams God has in store for us, but no matter what they are and where they take us, His blessings are our reward. Colossians 3 says, *Whatever you do, do it heartily, as to the Lord and not to men, knowing that from the Lord you will receive the reward of the inheritance; for you serve the Lord Christ.* And 1 Corinthians advises, *Let all that you do be done with love.* So, Elise, whatever you do, give it all your heart, and you will find goodness wherever you go."

"Do you think there's goodness here? In Green Hills?"

"I sure do," I promised. "Starting with a new brother or sister for you!"

Elise's face bloomed with excitement and she skipped off to catch up to her friends.

I stopped walking to wait for Mama.

Xavier Holland walked next to her, so I fell into stride on her other side, looping my arm through hers. I'd avoided them both, so effectively, in fact, that I sensed they feared talking to me, concerned I'd run if they said the wrong thing.

"It *is* spectacular," Holland allowed. "The sun beaming over rolling hills and thick vegetation make quite a statement."

"One cannot fault God's artwork," Mama added, which made me proud. A strict personal code might not make Mama an easy person, but it ensured that she remained true to herself, always.

"Certainly not," I agreed, hugging her arm a little tighter as we strolled. "His paintbrush is unmatched."

A welcome party waited at the bottom of the hill, waving and calling out greetings as the wagons arrived. They stood in an open pasture between town and the trail, which ran parallel to the buildings that formed the small community.

My eyes roamed from the buildings — wondering which might be the mercantile — to the prairie, to the herd of cows and oxen grazing in the open range. Then my gaze found and settled on what I'd hoped to see: Henry.

Like a magnet draws one object to another, his eyes lifted and caught me staring.

Almost lounging in the saddle, Henry spoke to the two men standing by Scout, but he didn't take his eyes off mine. The three men conversed a few more moments. One began walking toward the wagons, the other one turned toward town, and Henry nudged Scout into motion, heading straight toward me — and Mama and Mr. Holland.

Oh, Lord…

That's where my prayer ended because I had no idea what to pray *for*.

Henry reined Scout to a stop a few yards before reaching us. He dismounted, took off his cowboy hat, and hobbled the horse. Then he walked to join us.

My heart thundered. Tension snapped in the air like fireflies.

"Mrs. Williamson," he intoned, making it clear he wouldn't be cowered. "My parents would like to invite you both to their home for supper this evening."

"Please pass along our regrets—"

"*Mama,*" I interjected, admonishing her rudeness.

"—as we need to see to the wagon and supplies before the wagon train leaves in the morning," she continued with a pointed look at me.

"Pa's already seen to that for you, ma'am. He's sent a crew to help Mr. Bumpus situate the wagon behind your building and unload your belongings into the store and apartment above."

"While that is very kind, we might not be staying," she retorted.

"Surely you'll want to sleep in a bed and enjoy lodging with modern comforts while making arrangements to travel back east."

She couldn't argue with that!

"It will be several days, possibly even a week, before I have plans in place," Mr. Holland said.

Henry made a soft noise that illustrated his skepticism and distrust, but he didn't so much as glance at the other man.

"Henry," I said, drawing his attention. "We'd love to join your family for supper. Please tell your mother thank you."

He gave me a single nod, his eyes still too distant for my liking. Then he turned back to Scout.

"Lieutenant Commander Holland will be with us," Mama called to Henry's back.

Henry turned back, his face neutral to her snide tone.

"Whatever you like, ma'am," Henry said. He glanced from Mama to me once more before taking his leave.

Oh, Mama.

18

Discretion is the better part of valor.
Idiom used to say that it is
better to be careful
than to do something that is
dangerous and unnecessary,
Merriam-Webster.com Dictionary

*B*ite *your tongue. Bite your tongue. Bite your tongue. Bite your tongue.*

If I concentrated all my attention on repeating the command over and over in my head as we walked from our new house and store to the Davis's home on the opposite end of Green Hills' budding Main Street, then I couldn't blurt out what I *wanted* to say to Mama.

"How nice of Mrs. Davis to welcome us to Green Hills with such kind hospitality," I said to chip away at the ice block Mama had become.

Holland agreed with a noncommittal mutter.

Mama didn't say a word.

"I'm sure she's gone to a bit of trouble to make our first

evening in town a pleasant one," I said, trying a second time for civility.

Holland mumbled something.

Mama didn't say a word.

"My mouth is watering at the thought of a real meal, served at a real table, sitting in real chairs," I said, determined to win our unofficial battle of wills.

"And I'm *real* hungry," Holland added, looking at me with an eyebrow raised.

Did he have a personality after all?

"Yes," I agreed, addressing Holland and hiding a chuckle behind my smile. "I'm rather famished, myself."

At that, Mama's eyes snapped to me, a victorious gleam in her eyes.

I wished to say that sharing a laugh at a humorous comment didn't equate to undying love. It was possible to engage in a friendly conversation without marrying the man.

Bite your tongue. Bite your tongue…

I did just that, swallowing the words itching to escape my mouth: a terse reminder of Deuteronomy 24:16 which reads, *The fathers shall not be put to death for the children, neither shall the children be put to death for the fathers: every man shall be put to death for his own sin.*

Just as Mama had no responsibility for my actions — namely, falling in love with Henry — Mama shouldn't shun Mrs. Davis simply for being his mother. It wasn't Mrs. Davis's fault Mama hated the man I loved. And it wasn't anyone's fault I didn't — *couldn't* — love Lieutenant Commander Holland.

The verse goes both ways. A whisper materialized in my mind, one sounding very much like Papa's wisdom.

Mrs. Davis couldn't be judged for Henry's actions. Likewise, I could not be judged for Mama's. All the same, I prayed her manners and strict adherence to breeding and etiquette would override her desire to be churlish.

My worries were for naught.

A rabid dog would've been no match for Henry's family and their kind hospitality. Even a prickly bear like Mama had no choice but to respond to their warm welcome with pleasant gratitude.

To begin, the Davis home rivaled the new houses popping up back home. Not as large as those mansions, the Davis's two-level home shared an architectural elegance with stately homes in Back Bay and Beacon Hill. In particular, the common elements such as the use of brick and stone materials, a resplendent wooden entrance, and decorative ironwork trims reminded me of our previous community.

The inside took my breath away.

"I thought you said they sold everything they owned to come here," I whispered to Henry as he escorted me to the dining room.

"I said *most* everything," Henry said, correcting me with a concealed grin. "Which basically allowed Ma to start from scratch when they arrived."

"It's magnificent," I announced, no longer whispering.

"Ma has a talent for making four walls, a floor, and a roof into something beautiful and functional." Pride for his mother filled Henry's words.

"She does at that," Mr. Davis agreed. "As well as a staunch determination that Green Hills will develop into a prosperous—"

"And *progressive*," Mrs. Davis interjected.

"—town on the plains," Mr. Davis finished, flashing a loving smile and a quick wink at his wife.

"A bit of a job, I imagine," Mama said, a thread of challenge in her tone. "…with so few amenities and minimal population, not to mention the extreme difficulty in getting here."

"Charm and culture need not be exclusive of one another,"

Mrs. Davis replied with a gracious smile. "We have them both in Green Hills, and a blank canvas on which to design."

"God supplied a truly beautiful backdrop to work with," I said, tipping my head toward the window, through which the sunset displayed an explosion of colors resembling broad strokes of a paintbrush swathed across the darkening blue sky.

"That he did," Henry said, his voice heavy with conviction.

I glanced back at him, expecting his eyes to be on the horizon, sure that the longing in his voice resulted from his love for the land. Instead, when I turned, I found his eyes set on me.

"One finds an equal amount of beauty in civilization," Mama said, leaving no doubt where her loyalties lay.

"Oh, I agree," Mrs. Davis replied, her tone filled with wonder and animation. "It's all in one's approach, don't you think?" She projected her question in Mama's direction, but Mrs. Davis didn't wait for a response. "If one looks for the good in a person or a place, they will discover just that. By the same token, if one has predetermined to dislike a situation, more often than not, they create a self-fulfilling prophecy. Yes, it's all in what we hope to find. Why, even in a field of fresh snow, which at first glance appears cold and harsh and inhospitable, one can't help but notice how spectacularly the snowflakes sparkle while reflecting the sun or the moon, just like crystals in a decadent ballroom or stars filling the night sky."

"Is harsh and inhospitable snow common here?" Again, Mama's tone decried her less than optimistic expectations of a winter in Green Hills. Mrs. Davis's eloquent speech fell on deaf ears as far as Mama was concerned.

"We'll see some," Mr. Davis answered. "Nothing like the brutal months any of us experienced in Philadelphia or you in Boston, of course," he added with a gleam of suppressed humor in his eyes. "But the spring and fall make up for the hot summer and chilly winters."

"There's nothing so verdant and lovely as the spring and the fall here in Green Hills," Mrs. Davis confirmed. "How lucky you are to have arrived at the peak of the season."

Mama didn't respond. Had they rendered her speechless? *One could hope.*

I admonished myself for the tacky thought, and yet, I wholeheartedly enjoyed the delicate and polite way in which the Davises had essentially put Mama in her place. She hadn't given Green Hills a chance; she'd been determined to hate it before we'd even left Boston.

Before I thought of something meaningful to say, Holland *ahem'ed* to clear his throat. All eyes turned his way.

"This is a fascinating region," he declared. "Before setting out to locate Miss Williamson's wagon train, I studied maps of the area…to be alert and aware of the dangers we would face on the open range. The Ozarks to the north, the plains to the west, the Piney Woods to the south, and the Jackfork and Pine Mountains all around overlap to create a rather unique terrain. Mrs. Davis, you are correct in that the vegetation thrives here. With an abundance of rivers, streams, and lakes, one can surmise the hunting and fishing is fruitful as well."

"One might say we have it all," Henry offered with an undeniable air of impudence.

"It's as though God couldn't pick just one felicitous feature to highlight, so he cast them all upon this divine tract of earth," I said, delighted by the vision of our new home that their commentary painted in my mind. Enchanted by the moment, I smiled first at Holland and then at Henry, thrilled by our mutual admiration of Green Hills.

But Henry didn't smile back. His lips pressed into a straight line and his jaw ticked, creating a sour expression on his face. I questioned his displeasure with a tilt of my head. He must've recognized the concern in my eyes; he looked directly into them. Then he looked away, without even a blink.

"Have you traveled extensively in military service?" Mrs. Davis asked Holland.

Once prompted, the taciturn soldier went on to monopolize the conversation throughout the full meal. In a surprising turn of events, the quiet, stuffy man not only had a personality, he excelled at storytelling.

While sipping the first course, a scrumptious catfish stew filled with fresh tomatoes, potatoes, and onions and spiced with peppers, Holland retold a tragically funny story about his cabin mate the two years he served as an apprentice on the USS *Constitution,* better known as *Old Ironsides* and made famous to the American people after her heroic efforts in the War of 1812. During the main course of roast beef, which Mr. Davis carved at the table with quite a flourish, accompanied by ginger glazed carrots, pan fried potatoes, and bacon-wrapped green beans, Holland enthralled the group with stories of his life as a midshipman at the United States Naval Academy. Amidst a treat as incredible as Mrs. Davis's peach cobbler for dessert, Holland relayed the fascinating technology he'd helped develop in the realm of torpedoes while stationed in Rhode Island the previous three years.

"What an exciting life you've led," I commented, amazed at the transformation we'd witnessed, him growing with charisma with every tale.

"Where will you be stationed next?" one of Henry's younger sisters asked.

"That depends on Miss Williamson," Holland said, nodding in my direction.

"And why is that?" I asked, shocked by his revelation.

"I'm in line for promotion to commander soon. It comes with base housing. That is, if Miss Williamson agrees to live in military housing after we wed."

"You wouldn't have a proper house?" Henry's youngest sister asked.

"Not if Miss Williamson will move as necessary for my career advancements. Officers move frequently, going where they're needed, so base housing makes the most sense."

"And when there are children?" Mrs. Davis asked. "Are they—"

The scraping of Henry's chair across the pine floorboards garnered everyone's attention.

"*If* you wed," he said, correcting Holland's earlier statement with an icy glare. His pretty gray eyes turned into the polished-like surface of a steel sword. "I need to go feed," he explained to no one in particular before striding from the dining room.

"I'll help you with the horses, son," Mr. Davis offered before Henry reached the door.

"No," Henry barked. Then he cringed, obviously remorseful. "No," he repeated in a softer, more polite tone. "Thank you, but I've got it. Maybe you could look over those papers."

Henry avoided looking at me, but the message he sent rang clear as a bell.

The marriage contract — those were the papers.

No one said a word or even moved a muscle until a full minute after the door closed behind Henry.

Unable to sit under the oppressing silence, I folded my napkin and placed it on the table as I addressed Mrs. Davis with a grateful smile. "Please let me help clear the table." For all my bravado, my voice quivered and revealed the true extent of my nerves.

"That would be lovely," she said with a kind smile. "I'll stack the dishes in the sink if you'll combine the leftover roast and vegetables for tomorrow's soup. We have a root cellar to keep it cold overnight."

"Does that mean we don't have to help?" one of the younger girls asked, excited by the prospect of a night without chores.

"It means you may escort Mrs. Williamson and Lieutenant Commander Holland into the sitting room. You could each play a piano piece for them while we tidy up the kitchen," their mother instructed.

"Yes, ma'am," the two girls said in unison. They both turned expectant eyes upon Mama and Holland, effectively trapping the adults into following the children out of the dining room.

As soon as they left, I retrieved the villainous document from my reticule and handed it to Mr. Davis.

A nod of understanding passed between us. He simply *had* to find a way or a reason to nullify the contract.

19

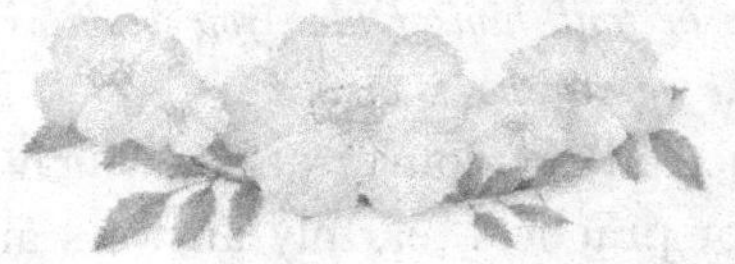

"Before the Next Teardrop Falls"
Song written by Vivian Keith and Ben Peters
Billboard #1 Recording by Freddy Fender (1975)

Day 14 ~ May 3, 1883

A heavy blanket of dread smothered me by the early hours of the morning. Throwing off my actual covers, I dressed quickly and snuck outside to walk.

And to think… Too many thoughts — conflicting, scary, frenzied thoughts — fought for space in my head.

I hadn't seen Henry since he left the supper table the night before. The moment each of his sisters finished playing a duet on the piano, Mama had called for me to join herself and Holland to walk back to the shop. Huddled over an open book and the contract, Mr. Davis hadn't even said goodbye, so absorbed in my legal issues he didn't seem to notice us leaving. He'd jotted down several notes on a piece of paper. I prayed that meant something good.

Although the clear, cloudless light allowed for plenty of

moonlight to guide my steps, I focused on the ground. *One foot in front of the other.*

Why did you sign that contract? Is a nomadic life from naval base to naval base what you wanted for me? Did you see something in Xavier Holland that led you to believe he would win my heart? Am I intentionally blind to your wishes because I want to believe you'd choose Henry, too? Shouldn't love be enough? Why put Henry in my path, why make me love him, if I'm not to be with him? Didn't you guide us to this place for a reason? Please make your wishes known.

So entrenched in my conversation, which flipped between begging Papa for practical, earthly answers and begging God for the realization of my hopes and prayers, I didn't hear or see Scout until I'd come upon him eating grass under the canopy of two majestic oak trees.

I approached slowly, letting the horse smell my hands before stroking his nose and jaws. He stepped closer to my touch, and I'd have sworn I heard sympathy in his affectionate nicker.

"I love him with all I am," I whispered to the horse, knowing Henry wouldn't be far from Scout and not wanting my words to reach him. "I thought he loved me, too."

"You know I do," Henry said, stepping between the two large trees.

My voice had carried more than I'd hoped.

"I *did*," I corrected. "But everything feels different now that we're here. You're different."

"I'm the same," he assured me. "I *feel* the same about you. But the situation has changed. Your mother only agreed to settling in Green Hills because she didn't have any alternatives. That's no longer the case. Now you have Holland, and what he's offering is…good."

"It is," I agreed, no longer keeping my voice down. My hands dropped from Scout. The horse sensed the shift in my emotions and stepped away, leaving an empty path between Henry and me. "It's stable, and predictable, and easy." I spat each adjective at Henry, agreeing with him point by point and step by step. My temper flared as I closed the distance between us. "I can be an officer's wife…Mama says maybe even a first lady. I can wear the finest silks and dress in the height of fashion. We'll travel the world, dragging our children from one military base to the next. We'll be polite. At all times, we'll present the image of a loving couple." Tears streamed down my cheeks. I couldn't say whether they stemmed from sadness at the picture I described or from the anger making my fingers itch to wring Henry Davis's neck. "But it will all be fake…because our life will be indifferent at best and cold at worst…miserable, and lonely, and loveless!"

I stood mere inches from Henry, steaming with frustration. To his credit, he didn't budge or back away from my tirade. Our eyes bore into each other's. I wanted — *needed* — him to say something. To fight for me. For us!

But he didn't say a word.

"It will be a tragedy," I said, "because I love *you.*"

Either my words or my broken heart finally pierced the barrier Henry'd constructed between us. He lifted his hands to my face, brushed away my tears, and tangled his fingers into my hair. "Don't ever — *ever* — doubt how much I love you," he said, searching my eyes for acceptance….acknowledgement… acquiescence. I wasn't sure which, but I understood, so I nodded.

When his lips descended to meet mine, I suddenly felt starved for him. I grabbed his wrists, his arms, his shirt… anything to pull him closer. I couldn't get close enough.

The more frantic my clutches, the more controlled Henry became.

When his arms wrapped around my waist and ribs to hold me in place against his chest, mine encircled his neck. Standing as tall as I could on tippy toes, I hoisted further and further into his embrace.

When I couldn't lift myself any higher, Henry lifted my feet off the ground. With a predatory growl and a half twirl, he backed me into the tree. His arms, tight with constrained strength, protected me from the rough bark of the trunk…so thoughtful and tender as his mouth devoured mine.

When I thought I might ignite from the heat of our passionate kiss, Henry grumbled an angry roar and tore his lips from mine.

A bucket of ice water over my head could not have shocked me more.

"Why?" I gasped.

"Because love is not enough," he answered in a raw, tortured voice. "Go live your life, the one you're meant to have."

The tree held me upright as I watched Henry lead Scout into the woods. Without the immovable support, I'd have crumbled into a shattered heap.

At some point, I did sink into a ball sitting at the base of the oak. I'm not sure how long I stayed just that way, but when the sun came up, I still hadn't found the strength or desire to move.

Go live my life?

My life had just walked away.

The rest of the day didn't improve, instead following suit with one painful goodbye after another. I reminded the children to read to one another and watch out for each other. I encouraged Margaret to believe in herself and trust in the plans God had for her future. And I traded recipes with Louisa and Sarah, so we'd never forget all the meals we'd prepped together — as if one could forget the people with whom they share life-changing moments. Mr. Rawes acted offended when I kissed him on the cheek and handed over a crate of canned fruit and jellies, but not so much as to refuse the gift. I thanked him for leading me home. Mrs. Moody gave me a stack of hymns to keep, and I gave her a quilt I'd made before leaving Boston. Mr. Moody said a prayer of thanksgiving for our safe passage to Green Hills and asked for God's continued favor as they traveled to Santa Fe. I said an extra prayer for the group I considered family.

After many hugs and countless tears, the wagon train pulled out after breakfast, taking an oversized chunk of my heart with them.

Mama let me wrap my arms around her as we watched the last wagon disappear over a lush green hill. "The store needs attention," she announced, wiping her cheeks. I took the hint to release my hug and dried my face, too.

"I thought you didn't want it anymore," I pointed out.

"Might as well set it up correctly for the next owners," she answered.

"Might as well," I agreed with a definitive nod. Then I clasped my hand in hers and we made our way toward Main Street. Mama held my hand the whole way there.

20

Deliver bad news early and personally.
Ron Williams

"Knock, knock?" Mr. Davis called from the threshold of the back storeroom.

"Please come in," I answered, covered in dust and glad for the interruption.

"This looks fabulous. You two really have an eye for creating the displays!"

Mama stood taller but didn't acknowledge the compliment, nor the man, for that matter.

"That's all Mama's talent," I told him. "I get too distracted by the goods!"

An odd sound, like a mix of credulity and humor, came from the corner of the shop where Mama arranged soaps and personal care products on shelves while ignoring us.

"I can see why; our townsfolk will be honored to own the merchandise you've brought. Thank you for that…for showing that respect."

"Again, the inventory is all Mama's doing," I praised.

"She's a forceful advocate that everyone deserves to know and enjoy quality products and pretty possessions." The object of our conversation seemed to blush, but she stayed on task.

"I hoped we could talk for a few minutes," Mr. Davis said. "About the marriage contract."

My heart dropped to my stomach.

"Yes, of course," I replied with trepidation. "We have a tea table in the front; will that be okay?"

"Perfect," he said obligingly.

"Mama, will you join us?"

She hesitated, and I could sense a tug of war taking place in her subconscious. On one hand, she didn't want to take part or give credence to his findings if they were not in her favor, but on the other hand, she absolutely did *not* want to be left out of the conversation.

"Shall we call for Lieutenant Commander Holland?" she asked…her way of accepting my invitation.

"I don't think that's necessary," Mr. Davis answered, following Mama and me into the front of the mercantile and pulling out Mama's chair at the tea table. "From all the legal precedents Henry and I found, this matter rests in Phoebe's hands."

"Henry?" Mama questioned. "Why should he have anything to do with the legalities?"

"Mama!" I declared, admonishing her snobbish, hateful tone. I'd already explained that Henry had earned a law degree from Yale. She was being rude simply for the sake of it.

Mr. Davis responded with more aplomb than I'd mustered.

"It's a fair question, Miss Williamson," he said, casting Mama an indulgent smile. "It's true I have more experience reading the law, but Henry's knowledge of current legislation and court proceedings far exceeds mine these days."

I adored the way Mr. Davis's chest puffed with pride when he said it.

"And what did you two determine?" I asked.

"It's an issue of consent," he began. "Technically, arranged marriages are still legal in America, and each state determines their own limitations on marriage contracts. But throughout the country, states now require mutual agreement from both parties to marry."

"My not consenting to marry Mr. Holland automatically nullifies the contract?"

"Your consent is not required for your father and I to know what is best for you. The Lord gave you into our care, and we're passing that duty to Lieutenant Commander Holland. Once married, he will see to your well-being," Mama said, in more of a declaration than an argument. In her mind, the issue was cut and dry, not even an *issue* at all.

"That's true," Mr. Davis agreed. "…to an extent. In traditional, church-ordained marriages and with common law marriages, coverture prevails, meaning once married, your husband assumes ownership and control over your possessions. But at the same time, most every state has now passed laws granting married women separate economy, so they can earn wages, own property, and even manage those assets in some places."

Mama *hmph'ed*, perhaps her way of expressing an *I told you so*, or maybe snubbing her nose at the thought of a woman managing her own life…ironic really, seeing that with Papa gone, Mama would do just that for the rest of her years.

"The catch is that you are of age to grant legal consent for your person, and you are unmarried. That means you have full rights to own land, a home, a business… And you are at liberty to conduct yourself and manage your possessions as you see fit."

Mama gasped with indignation at the mere thought, much less that Mr. Davis had spoken that truth aloud.

"I'm sorry, Mrs. Williamson, coverture doesn't take effect

until one is married, and Henry tells me Phoebe is twenty-one years of age…fully capable of determining her future in the eyes of the United States government."

"We are not in a state of the union," Mama purported. "We are in wild Indian lands. What law prevails here?"

"Mostly treaties," Mr. Davis answered. "Treaties between the Indian nations, the tribal councils, and the federal government, which have ultimate say over the territory. Like most settlements, Green Hills has established a local government of sorts, and we adhere closely to the legislation voted into law in the surrounding states of Arkansas, Texas, and Missouri."

"Those three states adopted this *separate economy* policy?" Mama asked, less venomous than she'd been up to that point.

"Yes, ma'am," Mr. Davis answered. "With Arkansas, alongside Tennessee, leading the way in many areas of granting women's rights."

"So the mercantile is truly mine? No one can take it away, or force me to run it a certain way?"

"All yours," he confirmed. "Unless you break a law, sell illicit merchandise, or allow illegal activity on the premises, of course." Mama huffed at his audacity to even suggest such behaviors, and Mr. Davis winked at me.

"And it's my decision to marry when I want and to whom I choose?"

"I'm confident in that ruling from any court within several days' ride from here."

"Oh, thank you," I gushed, turning in circles from wanting to do too many things at once. Unable to stop myself, I enveloped first Mama and then Mr. Davis in exuberant hugs. "Thank you, *thank you*," I repeated multiple times. *Henry!* "I have to find Henry," I exclaimed. "Do you know where he is?"

Mr. Davis's apologetic and sympathetic expression extinguished the hope and joy which had filled my body with energy.

"He's taking a herd to market in St. Louis for the Sharp ranch. Then he'll head on a buying trip to Wichita and Denver looking for horses and bulls. He'll send the stock back on the train, so I can't say when he'll return. He asked me to give you this." Mr. Davis pulled an envelope from his file of paperwork and held it out to me.

I looked at it as though it contained poison.

"He's supposed to show me around Green Hills. He told me all about Daisy Lake… He's going to take me fishing again," I stammered. "He said he loves me."

"I know he does," Mr. Davis said, urging me to take the envelope.

Still, I stared at it, afraid of what Henry'd written inside.

"Then *why?*" I asked in a voice so soft from desperation that my words became a plea. "Why did he leave?"

"Here, dear." Mr. Davis placed the letter in my numb fingers. "He wanted you to have this." Then he faced Mama. "Mrs. Williamson, please let us know how we can help you get settled." Mr. Davis tipped his hat and left.

Mama bustled past me to resume her work staging merchandise.

I stood frozen in place.

Keep going… One foot in front of the other.

My mantra didn't work.

Do something… You have to do something…anything besides stand here terrified of a piece of paper folded in a silly envelope.

I continued arguing with myself.

Just move!

The heated command broke through my trance.

I glanced at Mama but couldn't think of a thing to say. She didn't seem to need my explanation, anyway, so I released a sigh and headed outdoors.

My hands pressed the flattened envelope against my heart as I walked through the prairie. With each step, I prayed

Henry's letter said anything besides what I expected to find written on the page.

I meandered, thinking back on all Mr. Davis had explained about my consent, my choices, and my rights. I closed my eyes as I wandered, envisioning the life I'd had in Back Bay and the life awaiting me if I returned to Boston — or anywhere — with Xavier Holland. Then I opened my eyes to study the wide open space surrounding me…the green hills, rolling in soft rises and falling in wide valleys as far as my eyes could see…the towering, majestic trees, their thick green leaves creating dense canopies of shade…bees and butterflies dancing and fluttering amidst flowers of all shapes and colors, vibrant in bloom and sweet in scent.

After choosing a tree to lean against, I sat down and pretended to be brave. I slid my finger under the wax sealing the envelope and retrieved the paper folded inside.

It smelled like Henry, earthy and crisp. I held it to my nose and inhaled deeply, savoring the memories his scent evoked… precious moments of riding Scout together, of walking arm in arm along creek beds and lake shores, of being wrapped in his embrace.

With a heavy sense of dread, I opened the letter.

Dear Phoebe,

I owe you an immeasurable apology. I made promises to you I cannot keep.

My life is on the open range, and you — an angel among us mere mortals — deserve a world befitting someone so special.

Pa will explain how the law is surprisingly on your side at this juncture. Until you marry, you are free to study at Radcliffe, own property, and live your life in any manner you choose. That's a powerful gift, and one I hope you don't give away too hastily, whether it be to Holland or anyone else.

I pray the man with whom you share your life recognizes the treasure he's receiving and is wise enough to give you free rein even after your wedding. You'll do great things; of that I have no doubt. I can already see books attesting to the change you'll inspire and the impact you'll have on the world.

You've certainly affected mine for the better.

On your list of possessions, surely to grow exponentially in the years to come, remains my heart. It is yours.

Always,

Henry Andrew Davis

21

There was a roaring in the wind all night;
The rain came heavily and fell in floods;
But now the sun is rising calm and bright;
The birds are singing in the distant woods...
Poem: Resolution and Independence
by William Wordsworth (1807)

I was an emotional mess after reading Henry's letter, useless to anyone and miserable to be around. Mama spent the bulk of her day arranging the shop, still insistent she did so only to help the new owners, whoever they might prove to be. Mr. Holland appeared for supper after having spent his day— Well, I did not know where he'd been, as I'd spent the hours too absorbed in my heartbreak to notice or care.

Mrs. Davis and Henry's sisters had visited midafternoon, delivering fresh bread with the soup I'd compiled after supper the evening before. From where I'd been sitting — and moping — under the big oak tree, I saw the three of them walking toward the mercantile and our apartment above it. Mustering the energy to go greet them seemed too great a task. They stayed considerably longer than I'd expected, assuming Mama might be short with them. But when they'd come from the shop, both young girls skipped ahead, chattering over something colorful in their hands that they evidently admired. It was difficult to see from so far a distance, but I'd have sworn they had new ribbons. And when Mrs. Davis emerged from the doorway, Mama accompanied her onto the porch, chatting. And smiling.

By all accounts, they'd had a delightful visit. A twinge of guilt twisted my gut; I should've gone to say hello, especially as they'd been so kind to provide supper two nights in a row.

Mama, Holland, and I consumed the delicious meal with limited interactions. Mama frowned at my despondent melancholy. She asked a leading question or two of Mr. Holland, and he carried the conversation from there.

After I'd cleaned the dishes, I carried a cup of hot tea onto the porch.

Mr. Holland followed me out with a mug of coffee and settled into the rocking chair matching the one I'd claimed.

"This is quite a place," he commented. "I can see why you're hesitant to leave."

Was I hesitant to leave Green Hills? Or only unwilling to leave Henry?

I thought for a long moment, trying to identify the root of my glumness. The answer appeared, lightening the burden on my heart.

"I feel called to be here," I told Mr. Holland. "Right here," I said, perhaps more to myself than to him as I watched fireflies loop through the darkening night sky.

Crickets chirped and a faint evening breeze whirled through the trees nearby.

"This is home," I said. "I can't marry you, Mr. Holland." I

lifted my gaze to his, making sure he understood the certainty of my conviction.

He nodded, rocking in his chair and sipping his coffee.

"Will you call me Xavier?" he asked.

He chuckled when I looked at him as though he'd sprouted horns. Becoming more familiar with him was the exact opposite of what I wanted.

"You refuse to adhere to the Navy's title of my rank, and Mr. Holland is my father. His shoes I will never fill. So, it seems, Xavier is the last option for you to use in addressing me. Besides," he tacked on after a brief pause, "there *is* something special about this place. I feel it in the air, sense it in the land. I'd like to pass through this way again some day. It will be a comfort to know I have a friend to call upon when I get back."

He would not push me about the marriage contract. In fact, he didn't seem the least bit disappointed in the day's events.

I agreed to call him Xavier and gave him permission to call me Phoebe. We discussed the ways Green Hills might develop and how it could look when he deigned to visit again. I asked where he anticipated to be stationed next, and he described the path he hoped his career would take from there.

Mama was correct when she accused me of judging Xavier — of discounting him as a person as well as suitor — before giving him a chance. I'd done the exact thing I'd criticized Mama for doing.

After a brief and well-deserved internal rebuke, I gave Xavier my full attention and enjoyed talking with him late into the night.

An honorable and intelligent man, he'd make someone a fine husband someday.

It just wouldn't be me.

22

Rare as is true love, true friendship is rarer.
Jean de La Fontaine

Day 15 ~ May 4, 1883

"Why would you have married me?" I asked Xavier after breakfast the next day. He'd offered to dry dishes as I washed, and I welcomed his company. During the morning meal, Xavier had announced that he and his hired travel companions planned to leave before lunch, heading back to Van Buren where he could send a telegraph requesting new orders. "You don't love me."

"How could I?" he asked, a teasing note in his tone. With an indignant flair, I turned wide eyes his way. "I mean, I barely know you," he added with a grin.

"I thought I knew Henry." I'd avoided talking about Henry, tried my hardest to not even think about him.

"You do," Xavier said. "He'll be back. He'd be a fool to let you go."

"You're letting me go," I reminded him.

"You were never *mine* to start with."

Quite right.

"So, back to my original question. Why were you willing to honor that ridiculous contract our fathers signed?"

"Please don't take it the wrong way, but…obligation."

Ouch.

"My father was not a good man," he said, setting the cup towel on the counter and leaning against it to face me with his arms crossed across his chest. "He made life difficult, often unbearable, for all those cursed to be in his presence. When I was twelve years old, I enlisted in the US Navy as a Boy First Class. That put me on a brig where disgusting men whipped and mistreated apprentices every day. Still I preferred that escape over life in my father's home."

"You've only ever known the ocean," I said in amazement.

"*Hark, do ye hear the sea?*" he said, quoting Shakespeare. "It calls to me as these green hills call to you. Even in this land-locked territory, wild with the promise of danger and adventure, my body rocks to the rhythm of the waves."

"And yet, you would have accepted orders placing you behind a desk — on land…for me. You said so during supper at the Davis's house. You said with a wife in tow, you'd choose safer ways to command off the water."

"I'd have done so gladly. You see, my mother is a saint. A sweeter, gentler, kinder woman you'll never meet. And strong — In all my travels, she remains the strongest person I've ever encountered. She'd do *anything* to help *anyone*, and she'd happily go above and beyond for me. Doing so nearly got her killed."

"I have to hear this story," I said, intrigued. I pulled out two chairs at the kitchen table, gesturing for Xavier to take the one across from me.

He looked at his pocket watch before succumbing. "The quick version," he acquiesced.

"So I should grab a cup of tea?"

"Fine," he laughed. "But make mine coffee, and I'm not waiting to begin."

"I'm all ears."

"In the spring of 1859, I turned five years old, and I was infatuated with baseball. We lived in Greenwich Village on the outskirts of New York City, an eclectic part of the city budding with artists, immigrants, and the always fashionable wealthy. The sights and sounds of our neighborhood provided constant entertainment. My favorite thing to do was watch the Saturday baseball games that popped up in the park where my mother took me to play. That summer, my mother read a newspaper article to me about the first collegiate game which took place on July 1st between Amherst and Williams. She read the rosters to me, highlighting how many runs and outs each player had on the day. She explained the differences between Massachusetts rules and the New York rules I'd learned. The final score was 73–32 in Amherst's favor after twenty-five innings. We laughed together with amazement when she shared that following the baseball game, the two teams competed in games of chess, which Amherst also won. The newspaper billed the event as *a trial of the mind as well as muscle.* I can still hear my mother saying, *That's what I want for you, Xavier…a life that develops your mind as well as your muscle.*"

By then I'd heated our tea and coffee and returned to my chair at the table, utterly entranced in his tale.

"Four months later, my mother agreed to take me to a college game in New York City. It was November 3, 1859, and the Fordham Rose Hill Baseball Club team from Fordham University's St. John's College beat the team from St. Francis Xavier with a score of 33–11 in the first college game played under Knickerbocker Rules."

"What kismet…Xavier College played and Xavier Holland was there to watch."

"No, I wasn't," he countered with a grim expression. "My

mother purchased tickets, made a big deal about the outing being an early holiday present, and planned for us to enjoy the entire day in the city. My father, prompt to jealousy, decided if it was going to be that much fun, he'd come along, too. He was also quick to the bottle each morning, so when we left in our coach for the short ride into Manhattan, he'd achieved a good buzz. With a bottle to consume on the way, he'd transformed into a loud, obnoxious drunk by the time we arrived at the baseball field.

"He alighted from the coach first, whooping and carrying on. Just as my mother stepped from the carriage, my father smacked one of the horses with a stinging slap on the hindquarter. The spooked horse went wild and reared. The carriage rocked violently, in turn throwing my mother to the ground. She landed halfway under the conveyance. My drunken father stood frozen, neither reaching for my mother nor trying to calm the horses. Just as a wagon wheel would have sliced over her, a stranger swooped in. He pulled her from danger, taking the brunt of the wheel's weight on the lower portion of his leg. His fibula snapped on impact. Despite what must've been excruciating pain, he yanked all three of us — my mother, myself, and himself — clear of the vehicle without further injuries."

"Papa's leg," I breathed in astonishment. "It's what prevented him from being allowed to serve in the war. He only ever said it was a human's accident, but God's timing."

"My mother demanded we accompany him to the hospital where doctors set his leg and cast it in plaster of Paris. She further insisted my father repay the stranger's kindness in some significant way, having saved her life and possibly my own. There's no telling what could've happened to a small boy in a runaway carriage."

"It's too terrible to even consider," I agreed.

"Cheap and obstinate, my father refused my mother's

attempts to give your father something he might actually want. Heaven forbid my father might regret losing a prized possession. To appease her, my father gave away me."

"Pardon?" I asked, dumbfounded. "Did you say he gave *you* away?"

"Well, he tried. Of course, your father, being a decent human being, refused. So, my father said, *Have you got a daughter?* To which your father answered, *Not yet, but God willing, He will bless me with one someday.* You should've seen the glassy twinkle in his eyes."

"Easily brought on by the copious amounts of laudanum I imagine he'd ingested by that time," I teased.

"Oh no, your father loved you long before your first breath," Xavier assured me, prompting tears to form in my eyes in an instant. "To pacify my father, yours agreed to write that marriage contract. Once the two men had signed it, my father left it on the hospital table, dragged my mother and me home, and we never spoke of it — neither the incident nor the document — again."

"How bizarre that Papa kept it…for almost twenty-four years," I marveled. And then it dawned on me…

"*Mama,*" I thought aloud.

"Your mother wrote to me two months ago, explaining your father had died in a tragic accident, leaving you both unprotected and without the benefit of a male relative."

"She called the note due, just as Mr. Harden, our landlord in Boston, did on our building in Back Bay. She was sabotaging your life, just as he did ours."

"Sabotaging might be overstating it a bit," Xavier said with a laugh. "I'd have gladly married you, then strove to be a good husband, provider, and father to our children."

"All because Papa did what any man would do in that same situation?"

"Not any man," Xavier corrected. "My father didn't, and

if marrying you meant I could be like your papa instead of my father, I'd have been ecstatic to stand at the altar with you, vowing to do right by you until my dying breath."

His fist rested next to his still full, but no longer hot, coffee cup. I covered his hand with mine.

"But I can't marry you," I whispered. "Someone will be the luckiest girl in the world to be your wife. It just can't be me. You deserve true love, with someone devoted to you, someone who gives her whole heart to *only* you. And I've already gifted mine to another."

Xavier turned his hand palm up to hold mine across the table. With a nod of agreement, he smiled. It was a lovely smile, one that would certainly create a flutter in the right woman.

"She's out there," I vowed. "And I can't wait to hear about her! Remember, you promised to write from all over the world, so I can track your exploits and pray for your safety."

"Who knows? Perhaps you'll even meet her someday."

"We'll be kindred spirits," I said. "The best of friends."

When Xavier mounted his horse to leave Green Hills, I fought another bout of tears. So many goodbyes — too many.

"Lieutenant Commander," Mama shouted, waving a sheet of paper in the air as she strode toward the men about to leave. "Wait! You have to sign this amendment."

Xavier got right back down from his horse, looking at me for clarification. I had none.

"Mama, what is this?"

"Mr. Davis drew up an amendment to nullify the marriage contract. You can't marry him," she said, looking at me yet pointing at Xavier. "I can do this— I *will* do this… I will make this mercantile a success, and I will provide for us in a manner befitting two intelligent, capable women."

"*Oh, Mama,*" I gushed, so proud of her. "Of course you can. *We* can. And we will. I know how hard it is to imagine life without Papa, how painful every day without him must be for you. But together, we will make a new life here, meet new friends, and help this settlement develop into a thriving town. We'll make Papa proud."

"He's the only one who loved me just the way I am, exacting and strict and domineering. How many times did he tease me about ruling the world? I never thought I'd have to survive in a world without him. I didn't want this for you, this debilitating ache that threatens to crush me every second of the day."

"For the record, Mama, *I* love you exactly how God made you: honest and fair, tough and formidable, benevolent and true. And a safe marriage to a nice young man without the entanglements of love?" I proposed. "I agree it sounds perfectly fine on paper. But it's only half a life, Mama. And as I told you on the wagon trail, I want the deep, abiding, ceaseless love that you and Papa shared."

"Even if it breaks your heart and shatters your soul?"

"Even then, Mama. I want it all."

I wrapped her in a hug, smiling at Xavier as he signed the new paperwork, dissolving the last contract and freeing us both to follow our hearts.

23

Hurt people hurt people.
Adage of folk sociology;
Origins unknown but attributed to
everyone from self-help gurus
to religious leaders to random celebrities

Mama and I worked side-by-side straight through lunch. I cleaned windows, dusted shelves, swept floors, and beat rugs while Mama arranged products, staged displays, organized fabrics, and separated goods. We'd set our sights on opening the store to shoppers on Monday, so with only two days left to set up, we had no time to dawdle.

The light started to fade at the same time my stomach started to growl.

"Phoebe, grab a slip of paper and a pen. First, we need to list the most imperative tasks. Then, we'll devise a plan to be most efficient tomorrow and after church services on Sunday."

While I took notes, Mama heated the rest of the leftover soup, toasted slices of bread frosted with butter, and sliced

spiced peaches before putting them in a hot skillet. We
continued brainstorming ways to make the mercantile prof-
itable, shared design inspiration for the apartment over the
shop, tossed around ideas to decorate the front porch, and
envisioned how to layout a garden plot in the backyard. We
talked and talked, the way we'd done before Papa died…the
way we hadn't since then.

Although my heart ached, I went to bed that night with a
smile on my face. Mama had turned the corner on her grief.
She wasn't over it; a pain like that might never be *gone*. But
she'd chosen to grab hold of life again; she'd regained her
spirit.

Thank you, Lord.

Day 16 ~ May 5, 1883

A rooster's crow woke me at daybreak.

"We have chickens?" I called from my bedroom,
elated at the thought of fresh eggs every day.

Mama mumbled from her room, but I couldn't decipher
her words.

We stepped into the hallway at the same time, both dressed
for the day, and as they say, *bright-eyed and bushy-tailed.* Our eager
excitement hummed in the air.

Mama's smile went a long way to soothing the ache
Henry's leaving had caused. She looked ten years younger than
she had on the wagon trail — still made of sterner stuff, but
happy in her reticent way. I planted a kiss on her cheek before
she could shoo me away.

"We've far too much to do for all that silliness," she said,
ushering me into the kitchen for a bowl of oatmeal with brown

sugar and bacon crumbles left over from breakfast the day before.

"I wonder how far Xavier and his men rode yesterday," I mused between bites. "He hoped they'd make it to Van Buren and the telegraph office within four days at the most."

"I hope they don't run into trouble with the Indians or cattle rustlers. I should not have written to him with that contract." Regret soured her voice.

"I'm glad you did," I said, a rebuttal to her obvious self-contempt.

"But why?"

"First of all, I made a new friend…a dear one. I look forward to seeing the world through his letters. And he needs a bonus family, at least until he marries into one that will love and encourage him and his mother. In his line of work, I think one can never have too many prayer warriors thinking of them." I paused to take a bite, and Mama nodded her head in agreement. Now she'd be praying for Xavier, too. "Secondly," I continued. "I learned of another adventure in which Papa became a hero."

"He was always a hero," Mama corrected. "He just hid it most of the time."

"Too true," I agreed, pointing my spoon her way in emphasis. "I can't believe neither of you ever told me how he'd injured his leg. Or that you'd sold me in an arranged marriage," I added with satire.

"No need for drama, young lady."

"Third," I said, smiling at her teasing reprimand and returning to my list. "His being here helped you heal. Now I have my Mama back."

She wiped a tear from her cheek and returned my look of adoration.

"Remember that when you fall into bed exhausted after we work through that list we wrote last night."

Turned out, she'd spoken the truth into existence.

We unpacked merchandise from trunks and crates. We dusted every stitch of thread and inch of surface area. We arranged notions, folded fabric, and rolled ribbons. Mama set up the cash register while I set up the sewing machine. Then she hung premade clothing articles while I hung tools on nails to fill the side wall.

Mama allowed two breaks, one for lunch and one for supper. Besides those times, we didn't sit down the entire day. Before heading upstairs to cook, Mama and I stepped back to see the store as shoppers would.

"It's magnificent," I told her, threading my arm through hers. "Eye-catching with layers of colors and textures, neat and tidy so everything is easy to locate, and a perfect mix of wants and needs."

"I'll review the books tomorrow, but I think we're ready for Monday morning," Mama said. Her voice choked with emotion.

"He'd love it," I said, hugging her arm a little tighter.

Drooping over our evening meal and fighting to stay upright as we cleaned the kitchen, I blissfully climbed into bed with the first owl hoot of the night.

The hard day's work produced a solid night's sleep, which I welcomed.

Not only *didn't* I dream that night, I never even rolled over.

Day 17 ~ May 6, 1883

*N*o nightmares, no cowboys…*just sweet oblivion.*
     When the rooster crowed, I stretched with a colossal yawn. Then I curled into a ball, intending to sleep a

little longer, since Sunday meant a relaxed morning before church.

But going to bed so early led to waking early. Eyes wide open, staring out the window into the inky darkness before dawn, I gave up and flung back my sheets and quilt.

Rather than dress for church before breakfast, I pulled my quilt from the bed and wrapped it around me. I poured cold water into a mug to take outside and grabbed a decorative pillow from the settee.

A wooden bench, possibly an extra pew from the recently built church, ran nearly the length of the shop's front porch. I set the pillow beside the arm of the bench and propped against it with my legs out long, facing east in anticipation of the sunrise.

I closed my eyes and leaned my head back to rest on the wooden armrest when a soft, familiar nicker caught my attention.

Scout?

My heart sped up, but I refused to panic. Or hope.

I heard it again and sat up, twisting toward the sound.

Like a mirage in the desert, Henry stood in the street.

Not trusting my eyes, I fought the urge to rub them like a child on Christmas morning. When Henry began walking toward me, I gave in to the temptation.

Oddly, my hands came away damp.

These cursed tears…will I never run out of them?

Henry and Scout reached the hitching post in front of the porch; Henry looped Scout's reins over the bar. He stepped onto the porch and dragged a rocking chair to face my spot on the bench.

I pulled my quilt tighter around me. Was I erecting a wall for protection or chilled from nerves? I truly didn't know.

Henry sat in the chair with his feet planted wide. He took

off his cowboy hat and ran a hand over his head before leaning toward me to rest his elbows above his knees.

"You left," I said with a shaky voice.

"I'm back," he said with an equal amount of raw emotion.

"Why?"

"Phoebe," he said, as though my question was pure lunacy.

"For how long?" I asked, changing tactics.

"For as long as you'll have me," he replied. His tone issued a direct and definite challenge.

"You love the trail, living free under the stars…riding the range and driving cattle." I threw a gauntlet at Henry's feet; I couldn't be the reason Henry gave up the life he loved. To force his hand guaranteed he'd resent me down the line.

"It definitely has its draw. But it no longer holds my heart." Henry slid his chair closer to my bench, close enough to set his hat beyond my feet, which were still stacked at my side. "*You* hold my heart; it's all yours."

I swallowed but couldn't speak; my heart beat furiously in my throat. A wave of dizziness threatened to overwhelm me.

Henry smiled that secretive and sexy smile I loved. Then he slid my legs forward until I fully faced him and with gentle hands on either side of my hips, he moved me to the front of the bench so only a breath of air separated us. "I love you, Phoebe. I love *you* more than anything or anywhere. You are where I want to be, where I need to be… I can't give you a fancy life back east, certainly not the fine things he can—"

"I don't need them. I don't want them," I argued, finally finding my voice. "Henry Andrew Davis, I need — and I want — *you.*"

"Then let's turn all these *yous* into a *we.*"

"What?" I stammered as Henry pushed his chair back to kneel in front of me…in my nightgown, with bare feet, and cocooned in a quilt.

"Phoebe Victoria Williamson?" His calm eyes roamed over

my frantic ones. His lips lifted in a grin. He ran the back of his fingers down my cheek before reaching into his vest pocket to pull out a ring. "Will you spend the rest of my life loving me? Living right here on this land as my wife? Will you marry me?"

I think I said yes.

I know I whimpered, and I'm pretty sure I nodded while he slid the delicate band onto my finger.

Then I wrapped my arms around his neck and fell into his body.

He stood to counter my weight, which almost knocked him over, lifting me with him and holding me so tight that my feet no longer touched the ground.

I lifted my head to look him in the eyes.

"You'll never leave me again?"

"Never," he vowed.

"You've done it twice now," I reminded him.

"But I came back thrice."

That's a fair point.

"No more rejection letters because you *think* you know what's best for me?"

"You'll never feel rejected again," he promised. "Anything you want — it's all *yeses* from here on. I'll even forget the word *no* exists."

"Do you want to set me down?"

"No," he teased, nuzzling my neck.

"Are you sure?"

"Most definitely," he said in a huskier voice.

"Not about that," I chastised with a tug on his hair. "I mean, about settling here…with me."

I needed to make sure, and Henry seemed to sense the importance.

He leaned down until my toes connected with the porch floorboards, and he eased his arms from around me to ensure I had my balance.

Henry framed my face to look directly into my eyes.

"There is nothing I want more — nothing I've prayed harder to receive — than a lifetime of days by your side."

"I love you, Henry. More than I believed possible, and I'll love you for all of my days."

24

Grow old with me, the best is yet to be.
Robert Browning

*H*enry scooped me into his arms and sat back in the rocking chair. Nestled that way, we watched the sunrise and talked.

He'd only been gone three days, but I had tons to tell him. Henry hugged me tighter when I told him Mama had changed her mind about selling the mercantile. He growled in my ear when I explained how Xavier and I became friends and had promised to stay in touch. And he offered a heartfelt *Praise the Lord* when I told him about Mama breaking through her grief over Papa.

Henry rocked me as I shared how sad it had been to say goodbye to our friends on the wagon train. And he listened as I described all the work Mama and I had accomplished in the shop. Then Henry told me how he'd regretted his decision within an hour of leaving Green Hills.

"By midday, I'd become as prickly as a cactus," he

confessed, chagrined. "The men avoided looking my way for the daggers I glared at anything that moved. The herd was too big to simply turn around and come back. I stuck it out to the outskirts of McAlester. Then I rode into town and hired a drover to take my place. Scout needed a few hours' rest, so I rented a stall for half a day. With time to kill, I thought to look for a place to eat, but the first business I noticed happened to be a jeweler, just down the street from the stables where I'd left Scout. One look at that shop, and God's plan for me — for *us* — became clear as day. A devastating tragedy put you on that wagon train. Some pretty significant life changes, like my folks moving here and me switching careers on a whim, had me joining you. It was the Lord's path all along; we were meant to meet on that dusty trail, we're meant to settle right here in Green Hills, and we're meant to love one another forever."

I lifted my hand to admire my ring, twinkling in the new light of day.

Lacy filigree work decorated the gold band. A blend of pearls and diamonds set in a quatrefoil-shaped cluster surrounded a square-cut emerald.

"It's lovely! I couldn't have dreamed of a more perfect design. I love it," I told him. "And you," I said, placing a kiss on his cheek. Then another. And one under his jaw. I'd never been so forward — wouldn't have known how to be — with anyone else. But Henry gave me confidence, as though I could do no wrong, take no missteps. With him, love came naturally.

He purred in response, a sound that expressed pleasure and promise. A surge of power tingled in my veins. It fed my contentment, and I smiled with joy as Henry shifted me on his lap to nestle my head in the curve of his neck.

"It's used," he said, referring to my ring. "The jeweler said he bought it from a French actress in a theater troupe that rolled through town recently. Based on the design and how it resembles Queen Victoria's style in the early years of her reign, he estimated it to be close to forty years old."

"Think of the adventure it has seen. And now it's here…in Green Hills…with us."

Henry *mmm'ed* a quiet sigh and rubbed his cheek against my hair.

His breathing slowed, and within a minute, I heard a soft snore.

I watched the sun continue its ascent into the cloudless blue sky.

Thank you, Lord, for this beautiful day.

"You're smothering that boy in his sleep," Mama said, offering me a cup of hot tea.

"He rode all night to get here," I explained. When I reached for the mug, she turned my hand to examine the ring. "Henry wants to marry me." She brushed her thumb over the stones and then squeezed my fingers before sitting on the bench beside our rocking chair.

"I should hope so," she half-scoffed, smoothing a tear from her cheek. "The spectacle you two make…no telling what people will say today, you out here in a quilt and sharing a chair for all to see."

"They'll say I'm the luckiest girl in the world."

"And you're sure?" she asked. "Loving a man like Henry Davis comes with risks. Loving him unconditionally with every ounce of your heart, the way you seem to? That presents another level of potential heartache. Trust me… I know."

"I know you do, Mama," I said, reaching out to hold her hand again. "I'm sure. Because knowing the love you and Papa shared — even in such a brief moment of time as these past two weeks — has been worth whatever the future holds. We'll take care of one another, protect one another's love. I promise."

She studied my face, gauged the sincerity in my eyes. Convinced by what she saw there, she stood, but didn't drop my hand.

"Well, let that boy sleep…we have a wedding to orchestrate — today, before you ruin your reputation in its entirety."

"Today, Mama?" I stood from Henry's lap. "We can get married today?"

"I think you better," Mama said, holding back a smile.

I threw my arms around her, jumping up and down.

"Let's go shake out that ivory ball gown you were so set on hauling all the way out here. You'll be a stunning bride…really knock that boy's socks off."

"*Oh, Mama,*" I said, wrapping my arm through hers with a teasing nudge as we walked toward the door to the shop. "Henry's not a boy, though. He's a man through and through."

"We'll see about that," Mama muttered.

I glanced back at my groom to see a faint smile curving his beautiful, very kissable lips.

The prospect of a wedding at Sunday services created quite a stir, and every Green Hills resident showed up for church. The preacher, Mr. Randall, announced he'd resume the ongoing study of discipleship next week because the day called for 1 Corinthians 13, the Bible's *love chapter*. His wife, Mrs. Randall, fussed over a need for fresh flowers and sent a gaggle of youth to gather wildflowers from the fields.

We sang "Amazing Grace" and "All Things Bright and Beautiful." Mama shocked me by singing a solo in front of the congregation, a new hymn called "O Perfect Love, All Human Thought Transcending" from the sheets Mrs. Moody left with us. We partook in communion. And then Mr. Randall shared a sermon, ending with Genesis 2:24 — *Therefore a man shall leave his father and mother and be joined to his wife, and they shall become one flesh.*

He prayed over us and called us to the altar.

Mama stood by my side. Mr. Davis did the same for Henry.

"From Papa," she said, handing me a bouquet of buttercups.

In front of a congregation of strangers, in a brand new church, in a tiny, little town, I said vows to love and honor a man I'd barely known for two weeks.

And I couldn't have felt more at peace — or more at home — than I did at that moment.

"You may kiss your bride," Mr. Randall told Henry, and he did just that, draping my body over his arm.

"Ahem." Mr. Randall attempted to interrupt our first kiss as man and wife. It didn't work. "*Hmm-hem…mhmm-hmm-hehem!*"

Henry lifted his lips from mine, but only so far as to smile down at me. That mischievous, secretive smile and the twinkling gleam in his sterling-gray eyes melted my heart and claimed it at the same time.

Mine.

The thought struck out of nowhere, possessive and exciting and true.

"May I introduce Mr. and Mrs. Henry Davis," the preacher announced, apparently tired of waiting for us to catch up.

Henry returned me to my feet, but his eyes never left mine. He ran the back of his knuckles down my cheek in that soft caress that had become his signature sign of affection, as if he, too, couldn't quite grasp the fact that I was his…*to have and to hold, from this day forward.*

We shared an intimate smile, ignorant of our audience, until Henry's dad patted him on the shoulder and gestured for us to lead the procession out of the building.

When we stepped from the church steps, Henry didn't drop

my hand. Instead, he led me to an area of flat ground maybe fifty yards down Main Street from the mercantile. The sizable lot had been cleared, but weeds and grass sprouted in patches, trying to reclaim their habitat. Behind the lot, opposite Main Street, a thicket of trees opened to rolling plains, complete with a creek flowing through a flat valley between two gentle hills.

"Right here," Henry said, planting me in the center of the clearing and dropping my hand. He scoured the dirt, picked up a small stick, and began tracing long outlines. "This will be the porch — wraparound, if you'd like. And over here will be the kitchen, with picture windows to let in plenty of light. How about a parlor that stretches the entire width of the house? It'll be two-story; we'll put our bedroom on the second floor with the kids' rooms." He stopped drawing to face me. "How many do you want?"

"Children or bedrooms?"

"Either. Both!" I laughed at his exuberance. "Phoebe," he said with genuine, wholehearted sincerity. "I want to make your dreams come true, right here in Green Hills."

"You already have," I said, tugging the stick from his grasp and tossing it aside so I could hold both his hands in mine. "Everything else is extra. Whether we live here, or over there." I paused, waving my arm toward the far end of town. "Or anywhere. And no matter if or when we have children, and no matter how many arrive…everything will be bonus blessings. Because I already have it all. I am your wife. *That* is my dream come true."

"It has to be here," Henry said with a deadpan expression.

"What?"

"Our house — it has to be here," he said, gesturing to the outlines he'd drawn in the dirt. "It's ours."

"You own this land?"

"*We* do," he answered. "I bought it when Ma and Pa and the girls moved out here. Mr. Sharp negotiated with the Indians, instead of simply claiming homestead and stealing land from the tribes that lived around this part of the territory."

"You mentioned relations with the Choctaw nation are good; you told me about Aunt Jane, the wife of the Choctaw chief. That's why they will work with the settlers?"

"Exactly," Henry confirmed. "Having a parcel of land where my family planned to be seemed like a good idea, so I asked Pa and Mr. Sharp to select a location for me to purchase, one close to town but large enough to build a life on."

"That's what we'll do," I said, wrapping my arms around Henry's neck. "We'll build a life, and a family, and a town…on love. Our love, and it will last forever."

———

O perfect Love, all human thought transcending,
Lowly we kneel in prayer before Thy throne,
That theirs may be the love
that knows no ending,
Whom Thou forevermore doth join in one.

O perfect Life, be Thou their full assurance
Of tender charity and steadfast faith,
Of patient hope, and quiet, brave endurance,
With childlike trust that fears
nor pain nor death.

Grant them the joy
which brightens earthly sorrow;
Grant them the peace
which calms all earthly strife,
And to life's day the glorious unknown morrow
That dawns upon eternal love and life.

"O Perfect Love,
All Human Thought Transcending"
Hymn written by Dorothy F. Gurney (1883)
Song #158 from Christian Hymns:
for Church, School and Home (1898)

———

The End.

AUTHOR'S NOTE

In 2008, my family moved to Waco, Texas. A year later, the house was settled and decorated, the kids were active with school and sports, and my husband was busy coaching college football. After a full month of watching *CSI: New York* on repeat during the weekdays, I decided I had to do something constructive.

I've always wanted to make a splash, dreamed of doing something big and impactful. I wasn't sure what that *thing* might be, but I was an obsessive reader, an educator by profession, and I loved working with children. When I put that all together, I came up with a plan to go back to school in hopes of gaining some expertise in youth literacy.

In 2010, I graduated with a master's degree in Information Sciences (a fancy way of saying Library Science) and graduate certificates in Storytelling and Youth Librarianship.

Writing this book fifteen years later put that degree to good use!

It's my first historical romance, but it won't be the last... I had a blast digging into every little detail, researching life in America in 1883, and reading about what settlers experienced on the wagon trails. I'm a stickler for the truth and I love learning about past eras, so everything in Phoebe and Henry's love story is historically accurate except a few places where I took advantage of creative license:

◆ Radcliffe College was actually called "Harvard Annex" until 1894, but I bent the timeline to make the paragraph flow better.

◆ Most scripture is from the King James Bible, which would have been what they read on the trail. In a few places, I quoted the New King James Version instead, so the verses wouldn't be such a struggle to decipher as to jar the reader from the story.

◆ *The Pathfinder* by James Fenimore Cooper is quoted in several places and featured in *Phoebe*. Written in 1840, the novel opened my eyes to literature my characters would have enjoyed and served as an example for Henry's and Xavier's parallel pursuit of our fair maiden. *The Pathfinder* can be accessed in its entirety via the Gutenberg Project: https://www.gutenberg. org/files/1880/1880-h/1880-h.htm

◆ In Chapter 10, Phoebe performs the Heimlich maneuver, which saves a little girl in the wagon train. The procedure was not actually discovered until 1974, but I needed a way for Phoebe to work a "quick miracle" and a choking victim fit the bill perfectly. Read more about the Heimlich maneuver here: https://flushinghospital.org/newsletter/history-of-the-heim lich-maneuver/

◆ *Glitter and Glue: A Memoir* by Kelly Corrigan inspired the relationships between Phoebe and her parents. I would've loved to be the glitter, but that's Coach's role in our home. I'm fairly sure he's the glue as well. That's why Corrigan's book spoke to me so personally. It's about the way we perceive people we love but might not always *like*. That's a tough concept, but parenting — and especially mothering — is tough work. I appreciate Corrigan's journey to discovering that her mom's place in their family was vital and based in love, just like the role her shiny and fun father played. Published in 2014, *Glitter and Glue* is available in print, digital, and audiobook formats wherever books are sold.

Thank you for making it to the end of Book 7 in my ever-growing world of Green Hills! Next, we're headed to the present for an upcoming run of sweet and wholesome, modern day love stories before we travel back in time again for next year's Prairie Rose Collection. In the meantime, if you'd like more glimpses behind the scenes of my writing, please subscribe to my weekly-ish newsletter, *The Gazette*.

With love and hugs,

WRITER · QUILTER · ENTREPRENEUR

GREEN HILLS BOOK 7 PLAYLIST

Music is the shorthand of emotion.
Leo Tolstoy

Enjoy the music that helped inspire the story…

1. Cool Water - Sons of the Pioneers
2. The Wayward Wind - Patsy Cline & The Jordanaires
3. Cattle Call - Eddy Arnold
4. Prairie Polka - Denny Earnest
5. When You Say Nothing at All - Alison Krauss & Union Station
6. Fall on Me - NEEDTOBREATHE & Carly Pearce
7. I'll Fly Away - Gillian Welch & Alison Krauss
8. Safe in the Arms of Jesus - Michael O'Brien and Megan O'Brien
9. It is Well with My Soul - Joey + Rory
10. There is a Green Hill Far Away - The Lower Lights
11. He Could be the One - Hannah Montana
12. Annabel - The Duhks

13. Oh Mama - Milky Chance
14. Ashokan Farewell - Jay Ungar, Evan Stover, Matt Glaser, Molly Mason, and Russ Barenberg
15. That's What I Like About the West - Tex Williams
16. Where We'll Never Grow Old - The Lower Lights
17. All I Ever Need is You - Sierra Hull
18. Before the Next Teardrop Falls - Freddy Fender
19. Wondering Why - The Red Clay Strays
20. O Perfect Love - Slow Rising Hope
21. Happy Trails - Roy Rogers

———

Available on Spotify as
"Book 7: Phoebe
by Virginia'dele Smith"

ABOUT THE AUTHOR

Ashli Montgomery is a wife, a momma, a writer, a quilter, and an entrepreneur. Her passion is sharing love stories, books, quilts, yoga, recipes, and her favorite ways to create a lovely life.

Ashli writes wholesome and cozy romance under the pen name *Virginia'dele Smith* to honor Syble Virginia Tidwell, Adele Gertrude Baylin, and Etta Jean Smith.

These three cherished grandmothers taught Ashli to love without judgment, always putting family first. Through Grandma Syble's journals and appetite for books, through Momadele's priceless cards and handwritten letters, and through hours of visiting over fabric at Mema's kitchen island, Ashli also learned to treasure words.

Get to know Ashli by subscribing to her newsletter, *The Gazette*, at AshliMontgomery.com

**Welcome to the world of Green Hills
by Virginia'dele Smith**

Sadie & Sam: PART 1 - Introductory Short Story (FREE)
Book 0: My Manifesto - Short Memoir (FREE)

The Davenports
Book 1: Grocery Girl
Book 2: In the Trenches
Book 3: Three Times to Make Sure
Book 4: Take a Chance on Love
The Davenports EAT — A Green Hills Cookbook

Book 5: Undeveloped Love
A Christmas Collection Novella

Book 6: Stealing Kisses
A Valentine's Sweetheart Story

Book 7: Phoebe
The Prairie Roses Collection #50

***Ashli not only writes about
quilts, quilters, and quilting…
She's a quilter, too!***

When she's not writing, Ashli is often helping others complete their quilt projects through her longarm sewing business, Longarm Lucey, and *quilting to mend the mind* by connecting quilters with the fight to end Alzheimer's disease through Quilt 2 End ALZ, Inc., a 501(c)(3) nonprofit she launched in 2019, to use her quilting hobby as a platform to advocate for a world without Alzheimer's disease and other forms of dementia.

Learn more at Quilt2EndALZ.org

www.ingramcontent.com/pod-product-compliance
Lightning Source LLC
Chambersburg PA
CBHW010643190726
48289CB00009B/2828